ROSE'S WAR-1918

4
#2 of the Dupen Family Chronicles

By: Cindy Biggs Weiss

Read all the books in The Dupen Family Chronicles

#1 Forbidden Love, 1906
Elizabeth Dupen loves Johnny, piano tuner, from San Francisco. Her parents do not approve. How will the Great Earthquake of 1906 change their lives?

#2 Sam and Adam, Cowboys, 1912
Rodeo cowboys, jockeys and cattle barons, the Dupen boys are still up to their tricks.

#3 Jane's Story, 1916
Jane Dupen is a one-room school teacher in Siskiyou County, California

#4 Rose's War, 1918
It's WWI and Rose runs away to Palestine to help the sick and wounded as part of the Hadassah movement.

#5 Mary's March, 1920
Mary has moved to New York and is an editor. She discovers the suffragist movement and marches with them for the women's right to vote.

This book is dedicated to Henrietta Szold who visualized a Palestine of medical clinics and help for the poor and the sick. 1860-1945

Chapter 1

How much more must she endure of this boring class. Mrs. Blackstone's droning typing commands were going to instantly put her to sleep unless she could get her mind somewhere else...like the brave French soldiers fighting for their land against that mean German Kaiser Wilhelm. She wished she could magically fly off to France and see exactly what was going on. Flying, now there's an interesting concept. She knew the Germans were flying their Red Barons, but soon would airplanes start carrying passengers? Wow! Now this was something to wake up for. Imagine flying to New York to see her sister, Mary.

But now she was stuck in this typing class. Why? Why does she need to take typing? She would never be someone's secretary; no, not Rose Dupen! Her eyes were set on places far away from this provincial town of Chico, California.

Let Elizabeth be the writer of the family, she thought. *I'm going to be the traveling Dupen. First I'm going to Hawaii to meet Father's brother. I've got to find out for myself if he really is the scoundrel everyone says he is.*

"Rose Dupen," Miss Blackstone called out. "Are you with us today? Which is it, are you in Africa or South America this time?"

"Sorry, it's just that I can't see any reason to learn typing." That was Rose for you, always speaking her mind. "I'm not going to be someone's slave in an office somewhere."

"Oh, you are wrong about typing," she answered this rebellious student. "It is the way of the future for every woman. It is the best little machine to insure independence for the modern gal. Why Rose, however would you be able to submit your travel articles to some magazine or newspaper? Oh yes, typing is your ticket out into the rest of the world. Take it and run with it, Miss Rose Dupen...and the same for the rest of you. The job of learning to type may seem tiresome, but once you have this skill mastered, you will be able to ride the magic carpet to freedom. Now let's get back to our exercises... 'r space, e space, w, space...' remember, do not look down at your hands. Anyone caught looking will have three raps from this ruler I am holding!"

Oh drat, I suppose she's right. I am not going to stick around here any longer than I have to and traveling takes a lot of money. At least it will be a way for me to pay my way around this mysterious orb we inhabit. Ugh!

She felt something hit the back of her head. She turned around and there was Wyatt grinning at her. Not again. She had no patience with these childish boys. Just because he was best pals with Mark did not mean she would automatically like him. Having a twin brother could be good, and, it could be troublesome. Most of his friends were hoping to become her beau, but she was not interested in any of that. No. She wanted to be single and free to take the world by its tail and swing it over her head like a lasso.

She definitely was not like her older sister, Elizabeth, who spent most of her senior year pining for her Johnny. And, what a year it was, what with the 1906 San Francisco Earthquake and all. It's true she was able to maintain her writing career while being a wife and mother but she was tied to Chico or Sacramento where her editors were. She had managed some success with several articles finding national acclaim and she had also written a few children's books for her own young ones.

Mary, sister number 3, had flown the coop and ended up in New York City editing cookbooks, some of which she had compiled herself. But that was it....no globetrotting for her except to come back to Chico once a year.

However, it was Jane that had the pioneer spirit. She was living in Siskiyou County to the north and was teaching at a remote one-room school. Mostly, the students were from neighboring cattle ranches. It was a little strange for her to end up there with only those rancher types; she had never seen her as a cow-girl. But she seemed to be enjoying bringing some culture and book-learning to her students. She had mentioned in her letters home that her students were thirsty for anything to read and now she was asking for some of the books from the Dupen parlor shelves. So Mother and Father packed up the last of the kids' books and shipped them off to Montague, the nearest town where Jane was. Rose was looking forward to seeing her at her graduation later this month; they had a lot of catching up to do.

The strange thing was that Sam and Adam were the real cowboys in the family. They had left Chico right after high school and headed to Reno, Nevada to make their fortunes in the rodeos and horse racing and eventually branching into the cattle business. They did not get home very often since all their time was spent chasing either cattle or their young boys. Josh, Matt, Freddy, Jamesy, Robbie, and Paddy were said to be full of more spit and fire than their fathers were. Mother and Father try to visit them once a year and have come back with tales of the boys' tricks and capers that make their fathers' antics look tame. Mother often commented how she admired her two daughters-in-law for their ability to hold their families together.

This left Mark, Rose's twin, who sought the quiet, predictable life. She doubted that he would ever leave Chico. He and Bertha were already planning their wedding right after graduation, in May. Mark loved numbers and excelled in his math classes. He was working after school at Jackson Schroeder's office interning as an accounting assistant. He hoped to secure a permanent position there following graduation. To Rose, a life such as the one Mark had mapped out for himself seemed dull and too predictable.

I want adventure, excitement, freedom to choose where I want to go and what I want to be! She resolved as she typed away. She would be 18 later this year and it was time to get out and see what was percolating in the rest of the world.

Chapter 2

Rose and Ruth met under the clock tower as soon as the last class was over. This was their routine every day: meet at the clock tower on campus; walk to Driscoll's Creamery for a phosphate or lemonade; stop in at Dupen's Jewelry for a check-in with Mother and Father; head over to Rose's house to help with chores; and then over to Ruth's to start their homework; run errands if needed and then eat dinner. Finally, Ruth's father or mother would walk Rose home if it was dark. On alternate days, Ruth would stay at Rose's for dinner. Of course, in bad weather, all of this would change: umbrellas would be donned and they would forego Driscoll's and get to their own homes as quickly as they could, hopefully missing as many mud puddles as possible.

R&R (as they were known around school and home) were inseparable. As soon as Ruth arrived in Chico, 8 years ago, they both knew that they were kindred spirits. Often others felt that they were sisters except they did not look alike. Ruth was dark and shorter than Rose; Rose was tall and thin with auburn hair and a light complexion. Ruth's eyes were black, Rose's blue. No they did not appear to be related to each other at all. But when talking to them, their mannerisms and speech were identical. If they were in the same class at school, the teacher often mixed them up.

Dr. Eli Epstein, his wife, Rachel, and daughter, Ruth had arrived in Chico in 1910. They had lived for two years in Sacramento after Eli's graduation from Tufts Medical School in Boston. Upon receiving his degree, he wanted to move west away from the congested east coast. He was fascinated with the Wild West and vowed to move there some day. Rachel was not so sure about leaving her prominent Jewish family of Boston for the wilds of California, but secretly harbored an inquisitive nature and thought being a nurse to natives, Mexicans, ruffians, and the likes of Black Bart could be a great adventure. She had read the novels of Mark Twain and Bret Harte and longed to see where the famous gold rush of the 1850's had begun. She had read about it as a child, but seeing the Sierra Nevada gold fields would be exciting.

Eli and Rachel's biggest concern was to locate a synagogue in Sacramento. Was there much of a Jewish community? Of course, it just was a matter of doing a little research. Rabbi David from Congregation Beth Israel in Boston contacted friends at the Congregation B'nai Israel there and soon there was a passage of letters back and forth until their departure from Boston in the spring of 1908. Soon Eli and Rachel set up their medical office from their home on I Street. For two years they prospered, Ruth grew into an 8 year old, and many friendships were formed.

But the urge to travel soon hit Eli again and he wanted to locate in the north Sacramento Valley, precisely a little town called Chico. There was only one doctor and the town was growing beyond his ability to care for them all. He had met Dr. Fulbright and was enamored with the wonderful stories he told of Chico's charm and perfect weather and safe environs. Rachel especially liked that it was a town of roses and trees. She was intrigued with the stories of General Bidwell and his beloved wife, Annie. He had donated the land for the town and had designed and built most of it.

By 1910 the Epsteins once again packed their belongings, their medical books, medications and supplies and embarked on a new adventure. They located a home on 3rd Ave. with extra quarters and hung their shingle: *Epstein Medical Practice, Eli Epstein, MD., and Rachel Epstein, RN.* "Rose," Ruth called. "I'm over here. Come quick, there is a baby rabbit in the bush. But be quiet. I don't know where the mama is."

"Oh what a cute little piece of fluff," Rose smiled. It was spring and babies of all kinds were entering the world somewhere in Chico. The weather was warm today so a phosphate was in order for these soon to be high school graduates. The air was buzzing with wedding plans, military sign-ups, and college choices for the different members of the 1918 graduating class. The Great War in Europe was still on most everyone's mind, but soon it had to be over.

"So, Rose, what about your brother, Mark, is he still thinking of joining up to be a 'dough boy'?" Ruth queried. "Is the wedding still on? So many of our boys are signing up while they can; they really think the war is a great adventure. Don't they realize that death is not fun? Papa thinks soon Germany will be defeated and we can once again think about getting back to our normal lives. Imagine, Rose, no more bandages to make! Mama says the Hadassah in Jerusalem is still begging for more. I can't wait for this stupid thing to be over with. I hate folding bandages every night. Now she wants a group of us girls to come over to our house for a bandage making bee. She's calling it the 'Bandage Bee'. She says it will be like a quilting bee, only without the pretty designs, just plain old bandages. But I guess I should not complain. However, I would rather be over there helping to use the bandages than over here making them. At least I would know if I was doing some good. Oh God, there's that Wyatt again. He really has it bad for you, Rose. C'mon, let's get out of here!"

Ruth took Rose's hand and they hurried off together with Rose barely having a chance to answer Ruth's questions.

Today they ordered a strawberry phosphate, and as usual, asked for two straws. "To answer your questions, Ruth, Mark is getting married, yes, and is leaving for the army after graduation. Mother is beside herself with worry, but Father thinks it is grand his youngest son has a heart to fight the Kaiser. This would make the last of my brothers to join. We haven't heard from Sam and Adam in a while and Stephen and Alfred are behind the lines in France decoding German secrets. I guess it is a pretty safe job, so I am told. I don't see how anything could be safe in a war. That is the exciting part, I think; to have such an adventure. I wish I could go instead of Mark. He would be some fighter with his nose always in the books. I, on the other hand, would be a great soldier. If I couldn't shoot or bayonet the enemy, I would, kick, scream and bite them until they all disappeared."

"Oh Rose, that is funny. I can just see you on the ground hanging on to some soldier's leg having yourself a grand meal just like it was Thanksgiving!"

"Oh, I forgot to mention," Ruth continued, "this year for Pesach, we are going to Sacramento to have Seder with some of our old friends. I truly wish you could come with us. Having you along would be keen. I'm asking Mama tonight if you can come. You *would* like to come, wouldn't you?"

"Of course, Ruth, I'll be your pal for Passover. But you will have to remind me what we are celebrating...I've forgotten."

"You know, it is the exodus from Egypt by the Jewish slaves of Pharaoh. Remember the seven plagues: the toads, the locusts, the river turning to blood...and the Pharaoh still would not set them free. Finally the last plague, the killing of every first born child convinced Pharaoh to let the Jews go free. Remember how the angel of death came to the people and killed the first born, even Pharaoh's precious boy? But the angel of death passed over the homes of the Jews who had painted fresh blood over their door frames. Then the Jews took off, came to the Red Sea and were afraid they would drown but the water parted enough for them to walk over to the other side. When Pharaoh's army tried that, they were immediately drowned."

"Oh sure, I remember now. That is the best Bible story of all, I think. But, then there is Jonah being swallowed by the whale, that's pretty good, too; oh, and the talking donkey story was funny. So, when do we go? You know how much I love to travel."

"Pesach this year falls on Thursday March 28th, so we will begin our travels the day before. Wouldn't it just be grand if you could come?"

"My land, it would. Oh my yes! I will welcome anything or anyone who can deliver me out of Chico. I'm ready to put on my hiking boots and hit the trail...proverbial trail, that is. I'm not into hard work, you know; just a nice train or ferry ride here or there. Say, I have an idea. Perhaps we can shop for our graduation dresses while we are in Sacramento. Mother says I may pick out my own. I've saved some money, and she said they will match what I have. We can stop in at the Dupen Jewelry Store there that my brother, Stephen, owns and find an exquisite trinket to wear in our hair. Oh, this will be such fun. We two will be the belles of the graduation ball."

Chapter 3

Everything was set. Tomorrow they would catch the train to Sacramento. Rose had packed her three satchels and Mother had packed her a small basket of snacks and sweet breads. Mrs. Epstein had been over to the house a few times to confer with Rose and her parents to make sure everyone was comfortable with Rose traveling with them and partaking in this important celebration.

Mother and Father were happy to be in the Epstein's circle of friends for it was Dr. Epstein who had saved Elizabeth's life while she was giving birth to Peter. Eli Epstein and his family had arrived in Chico with the latest in procedures, and new medicines. Dr. Fulbright was scheduled to deliver Elizabeth and Johnny's first born, but she began labor early while he was out of town at a medical conference in San Francisco. Everyone had heard of the arrival of the new doctor, but since Dr. Fulbright had always been the town's MD, it was hard to go to a new one.

Mother sat with Elizabeth during the beginning of her labor trying every potion and herb tea she could think of to stop the contractions. Nothing worked. This baby had a mind of its own and was ready to enter the world. Then the worse turn of fate happened. Mother could not control the bleeding. Finally they called Dr. Epstein as things were out of control.

From the beginning, Mother and Father felt that Eli was a God-send. He was calm; reassured Elizabeth he had seen this type of situation before; and was confident he could get her back on the right track that would bring forth this little baby with no trouble. He administered several new potions now being used in the larger cities. He gave her a pain reliever and Elizabeth was soon relaxed and drowsy. Her distress had alleviated considerably. But, this new doctor was still having difficulty controlling the bleeding.

It was approaching dangerous proportions and he knew he had to act fast. He quickly applied some new methods that had worked quite well on the battlefields where run-away bleeding was common. He worked with speed, dexterity and confidence and not once let on how very worried he was. Eventually, Elizabeth realized that she was becoming weaker. Eli called for hot wine with ginger and they were able to get her to drink it. Between the pressure from the poultices, tourniquets and this stimulating drink, the bleeding began to abate.

Mother and Father were so impressed with his skill, devotion and brilliance that they took him and his family into their circle and treated them like another family of Dupens. They would forever be in his debt and aimed to show the Epsteins a lifelong loyalty.

Yes, the Dupens were happy that Ruth and Rose were good friends.

They boarded the train at 10:15 a.m. and it was not long before they heard and felt the chugging of this fire-breathing monster moving forward towards Sacramento. They passed over the Sacramento River and moved down the Sacramento Valley through the rice and wheat fields. R & R sat together hugging the window in order to not miss a thing. They passed cows, horses, deer, eagles soaring next to the train, beaver dams in the river, and a lot of river birds. They were not bored and did not even think about the books they brought along to read.

Ruth had packed her favorite novel by Louisa May Alcott, *Little Women,* and Rose brought her book about Hawaii. She was still planning to go over there to find Father's brother. The problem was going to be in persuading her parents that she could manage by herself. She would advertise in the Honolulu papers for a job as a nanny and then start her journey to see the world with this as her first port of call. It wasn't as if she had never taken a cruise before. Several times the family traveled back to England to visit their grandparents and numerous cousins. She knew she could do it. The trick would be to convince them that she could. It was an exciting world out there and she was meaning to see it all.

She figured she had the same traveling and adventure bug that Mother and Father had. Right after their wedding, they discovered that Frances, Father's brother, had run off to America with all the heirs' inheritances. He was hopping mad, so along with his other brother, Henry, his wife Clara, and Mother, they followed the scoundrel to 'The New World' of America. They crossed the country sniffing out his trail of bad deals and angry partners until they found him in Chico.

He was there, alright, running a saloon and making one shady deal after another. Father demanded the deed to the saloon, sold it, and sent Frances on his way. Last Henry had heard, he was making more trouble on the islands of Hawaii. Father thought that having an ocean between the two of them was just fine.

Then, Henry and Patrick Dupen built their lives in Chico. Father opened Dupen's Jewelry Store, and Henry and his wife ran the Hotel Diamond. Clara passed on when Rose was still quite young, so she did not remember her, but the others said that she was so beautiful that she looked like royalty. Unfortunately, they did not have any children, so the Dupen children of Chico never had the pleasure of playing with any cousins unless they were on holiday in England.

Oh, she knew all of the Dupens now and there was not one that she did not like. So what could be so bad about Frances? Besides being a liar, cheat and thief, she couldn't see why she shouldn't get to know the black sheep of the family.

"I'm hungry, Rosie," Ruth broke into her thoughts, "let's move to the parlor car and eat our lunches that we brought. If we put them together, we should have quite a banquet."

"Where are your parents?" noticing their empty seats.

"They saw some friends in the next car up and have gone there for a bit of a visit. C'mon, hurry, so we can get a table before it gets too crowded."

"Isn't it just glorious, Ruth?" Rose giggled as they sat down at an unoccupied table. "Here we are rolling down the rails at a high speed, and we are merely going to sit down and take our lunch as if nothing is passing by us in a blur. The modern world is incredible."

"Besides that," Ruth added. "The aero plane has entered our lives and I predict that soon we will be able to travel back and forth across this fine land by resting comfortably inside one of those things. I think we are living in such exciting times. I want to explore too, Rose. Let's travel the world together. We will be partners as we visit exotic towns and villages in India, Africa, Egypt, oh...and what about Japan? I would love to see all of the Orient. I am thinking that I would like to travel with you to Hawaii after graduation. I can earn the money by putting in more hours at the clinic."

"I would be delighted to have you as a traveling partner. Four eyes instead of two are much better for seeing the world. We can keep journals and then compare them after we finish with each adventure. We would each have a different perspective of what we had experienced."

"Yes, and then we can combine them and create a book for your sister, Mary, to publish," Ruth was getting more excited and louder as she spoke.

"Mary only publishes cook books, but I would think that she could put us in touch with someone in New York who could help us out," Rose answered. "But I will tell you right now, my dear friend, that we will meet many who will not understand why we want to wander the world instead of becoming a teacher or nurse, and then someone's wife and mother. That is just not me, Ruth. I aim to shoot for the moon, and even if I miss, I'll still land among the stars."

"And I'm not far behind you, my astral voyager, not far at all!" and they both sat, gazing out the window and devouring their honey cakes like they were on safari and this was their only meal for the day.

Chapter 4

They had arrived at the Cohen's the day before the celebration of Passover began. Rose loved the family instantly. They were from New York, and, like Ruth's parents, had come west to work in the medical community.

Dr. Daniel Cohen specialized in eye problems and Anne was a nursing professor at the Sacramento School of Nursing. If ever Rose wanted to become a nurse, she knew that she would want to have Mrs. Cohen for a teacher; she was pretty, kind, and full of fun. Their children were Faye, 18; and the twins: Noah and Benjamin 12. It was the twins who kept the family on their toes as they were in and out of mischief on an hourly basis.

At the *Seder* (Passover meal) the next night, the two families gathered at the large dining table and Rose was formerly introduced to the world of Jewish music, and wonderfully prepared Passover dishes. There were new names for her to learn: *gefilte fish* (fish balls), chicken soup with *matzo balls* (dumplings made from special flour called matzo meal), *potato kugel* (vegetable egg pudding), *matzo farfel* (Middle East grain casserole), *macaroons* (coconut, sugar and eggs cookies) and *matzos* (an unleavened cracker made from the matzo meal).

One of the customs of Passover was to not eat any bread or wheat that had any leavening agent in it like yeast or baking powder to make it rise. The idea was to remember the Israelites who were fleeing the Egyptian Pharaoh and did not have time to bring any leavened bread with them. While wandering the desert in search of a new home, the only bread they had was *manna* that fell from the sky. Daily it was gathered and made into flat bread that had no leavening. In remembrance of that time, all Jews at Passover were instructed to not eat anything that was like regular bread.

Dr. Cohen led the *Seder* (order of the meal) and there were a lot of special things they did to remember the trials of the Jews at that time. One of them was to dip a spring herb, like parsley, into salted water to remember the tears that were shed during that terrible time. They had *horseradish,* which Rose loved and could not seem to get enough of, to remember the bitterness of the times; a lamb bone which stayed in a little dish for all to observe so they could remember the lamb that was sacrificed for the blood to paint on the doorways so the *angel of death* would not take their first-born child.

The story of Moses and the Israelites escaping the Egyptian Pharaoh was exciting to hear. Dr. Cohen told the story like he was there and knew everything that had happened and how scared and frightened they were. But in Rose's opinion, the best dish was the *charoseth* made from chopped apples, cinnamon and wine. It represented the mortar used when the Jewish slaves were building the Pharaoh's pyramids.

There were many parts to the *Seder* and each was accompanied by a glass of red wine. Finally, the main meal was served and there was an abundance of beef brisket, fruits, vegetables and sponge cake. There was merriment when the children were set to the task of finding the hidden matzo cracker, and lastly, the evening ended with the singing of the traditional songs. Rose did not understand them, but she hummed the melodies that hauntingly spoke of a time so long ago.

Soon the children became heavy lidded and begged to be excused to their bedrooms. The adults stayed awake for several more hours reminiscing over other Passover celebrations. They missed the families they had left behind on the east coast, and they especially missed the wonderful cooking done by their *bubbes* (grandmothers). It was a happy time, but a sad time, as well.

R & R shared a bed in Faye's room, the twins were next door, and both were upstairs in this downtown home on K Street. Dr. Cohen's office was next to the house in a separate one-story building that was once a garage for a wagon, and then later, an automobile. They were close to the shops and parks and were planning to explore all that the next day.

"Girls," Faye offered. "I just want to warn you that the twins are known to sleepwalk and that we might just get a visitor or two in the middle of the night," Faye cautioned. "If they wake you, just tell them to go back to bed. I'm telling you this because it usually happens when we've had company and there has been a lot of celebrating."

"Oh okay, Rose has a lot of experience in that department. She has 9 siblings," Ruth smiled and said.

"Wow!" Faye gasped. "You must have a lot of fun with all those critters to bug you!"

"Not anymore. You see, my twin, Mark and I are the only ones at home now. Mother was pregnant one last time when we were 7 but she lost the baby. I think it was just as well since she had her hands more than full with all of us Dupens. Now she just loves playing with the grandchildren. But I like your brothers; they are funny and fun to be around. They really know how to make a stranger feel comfortable. Actually your whole family does. Oh, and I thank you for sharing your room with us too."

"Ditto to that," Ruth chirped. "By the way, what are *your* plans after graduation, Faye?"

"I've been dreaming about graduation for a long time so I can get on with my life," Faye said confidently.

"So, it doesn't sound like you are planning on marriage now," Ruth asked.

"Oh my no, most in my class are planning their summer weddings and I am happy for them, but it is not what I want yet. I want to help people. I hope to marry someone who feels the same as I do. Eventually, I would like to set up a clinic to do just that." Faye nodded her head as if in resolution to this idea.

"What, no beaus to take you to the graduation dance?" Rose laughed.

"Heavens, of course I am going," Faye laughed. "Martin Feldstein asked me already. I did not say 'yes'. I said that I would get back to him after I consider my other offers. Of course, I don't know if I will get any more, but I do not want him to think that he is the only fish in the pond."

"Oh my, you are a trickster, Faye. Now I see where your brothers get their ways!" Ruth giggled.

"I just see it as playing our cards right so that we girls can get the best of the best," she answered.

Chapter 5

Rose was the first to hear the door creak open. *Oh those boys are here to take their midnight run,* she thought to herself. The moon was brightly shining and soon she could see that the creaking door was caused by something other than two boys who were sleep-walking. She sat up in bed and nudged Ruth. No luck there, as she was in a deep sleep that probably an earthquake would not disturb. *Wait, what's that? This seems strange. There are two creatures coming through the door and they do not look like 12 year boys!*

"Yeeee Gods! Who goes there?" she whispered loudly.

She heard a groan and in came two beings looking very much like ghosts. She covered her head with the sheet and groaned. It was then that she put 2 and 2 together and realized that Faye and her brothers had just cooked up a dandy plan to scare the two girls from the country. She would play along with it for a while. She acted as if she was trembling and moaned again. Loudly, she whispered, "What do you want?"

One of the ghosts in its white sheet said in a low raspy voice, "Tramp, tramp goes our soul, looking for a home in which to live, looking for just a little home. Where will it be? Whose soul can we take for our own?"

Then they shuffled around the room bending over each bed. When they came near Rose, she lay very still so that they would think that she was asleep. They bent over her and as they did she quickly snatched them from out from the sheets and revealed Noah and Benjamin.

"Ha! I caught you! Sleepwalkers, my foot! Noah and Benjamin, consider yourselves warned."

"Argh!" they both coughed up. "We can't breathe, let go of us, you octopus! How did you know it was us?"

"Oh, I didn't grow up with two older brothers who were tricksters for nothing. I think I have seen every trick in the book. Now Ruth, here, that's another matter. She's dead to the world and not aware that she just got spooked."

"Oh no I'm not, and this is what you get!" she grabbed both boys and brought them down to the bed. "Help me Rose....it's the tickle monster whom you are messing with now!"

"No, no....no fair, no tickling...I hate that!

"Ditto that from the twin! Help! Faye, save us!"

"I'm here, I'm here! I'm just having a grand time listening to all this. I think I'll settle back and enjoy the antics."

The noise in this tiny room reached such a pitch that soon they heard a knocking on the floor. "Did you hear that? What is it?" Rose asked.

"Not to worry," Faye said calmly. "That's just Father giving us a warning that we need to go to sleep. We get two more of those before he comes upstairs. You're good, keep it up girls!"

"What about us, your wonderful brothers. Don't you care that we are being tortured, here? Ohhhhh, hucka, hucka! We give, we give, honest. No more ghosts for you."

"You had better mean it or you will be getting some of your own medicine right back at you," Rose promised.

"Ok, ok," they said. "But you have to admit that you were kinda scared, right?"

"Me? Never in a million years; I knew you were comin'. That was a mighty fine set-up Faye if you ask me. Sleep walking? Did you think that we would believe such nonsense?"

"Well, the boys promised a day's worth of chores if I did it for them. I couldn't pass up watching them wash the dishes after supper tomorrow night. I can just see them with soap suds up to their elbows. That would be a sight and hey, boys, don't think I'm letting you off. You still owe me one night's dish washing, I'm collecting!"

"Aah, (yawning), I'm really tired now. Enough, and let's take this up tomorrow," begged Ruth.

"I'm with you," Faye chimed in.

"Me, too!" Rose agreed. "We have a big day of shopping tomorrow, right young ladies?"

"Well we will just shuffle down the hall now girls. Nighty-night, ta-da, and all that. Oh, and we hope the bed bugs *do bite!*" And off went the two Cohen pranksters to plan some more surprises.

Chapter 6

"So, what was all that about, Daniel?" Anne queried. "Are the children behaving?"

"I would say that everything is perfectly normal for three girls in one room. I just gave them the first warning to settle down and get to sleep. I'll probably need to go back up two more times before they actually do. Children... doesn't matter how old they are, it is still a chore to get them to sleep, eh, Dr. and Mrs. Epstein, wouldn't you say?"

"Ditto and ditto to that. Our Ruth and Rose are like sisters. If they are not at our house, then they are at Rose's. I don't know how they manage to maintain their high grades with the small amount of sleep they get," Rachel shared. "They really are attached at the hip, those two. I don't know what they will do after high school when they begin to go their separate ways, like college or marriage."

"My opinion," added Eli. "Is that those two will figure out some way to stay in touch, if not actually follow each other halfway around the world. They are both civic minded and have a heart for the poor and unfortunates."

"Speaking of unfortunates, Eli, have you heard the latest with Henrietta Szold's Hadassah movement?" asked Daniel.

"No, what is she up to now?

"Do you mean the Henrietta Szold from New York who spoke at Temple Emanu-El about the Zionist movement that is trying to improve the living conditions in Palestine?" Anne perked up in her chair. "I remember her. She was an inspiration. I'll never forget her words, *'The time is ripe for a large organization of women Zionists.'* If I wasn't already a wife and mother, I would have followed her right then and there."

"Yes, I have heard of her accomplishments," Eli commented. "It seems that she transformed the Daughters of Zion Study Circle into the largest Jewish women's organization in America."

"That's right," added Rachel. "Their motto is taken from the Prophet Jeremiah, '*the healing of the daughter of my people*'."

"She is asking for a group of doctors and nurses to go to Palestine to help set up clinics for the war refugees," Daniel explained. "I've not told Anne, yet, but I would like to be part of that group. I imagine that there are many children who have fallen victims from the war. I think I could be of some help. I was wondering if I could interest you, Eli."

"Hold on there, why just Eli?" countered Anne. "I would like to go too," Anne countered. "In fact, Rachel, you should go as well, and now that I think about it, this would be a great experience for the girls. I'll just arrange to have the twins stay with my sister in San Francisco. Let's do it!"

"I had no idea that you would be interested, Anne." Daniel smiled at his wife. "Why that would please me very much if we could all go together. Perhaps we could pool our talents and be of a great use in easing the suffering there."

"Well," Eli cleared his throat. "This is sudden. I haven't heard too much about Hadassah other than the drive to send bandages to Palestine. Do you have any printed material that Rachel and I could read? Let's continue this conversation later, it does sound intriguing."

"I agree, Eli," Rachel concurred. "I really do not know too much about the Hadassah movement, but I am definitely interested."

"Fine, fine," Daniel rose and went to his study and returned with a folder of articles that he handed to Eli. "Here, take these. You will become inspired after you read them, I guarantee it!"

"Meanwhile," he added, "how about some coffee Anne? I will get the Parcheesi game; everyone up for a few rounds before bed?"

Soon there was laughter from the downstairs wafting upstairs into the children's rooms. The girls giggled as they contemplated the idea of sneaking down stairs and telling the parents that it was time for them to go to bed as they were making much too much noise!

Chapter 7

Shopping in Sacramento seemed like going to a foreign country. They visited the Mexican Market, the China Market and the Jewish Bakery and Delicatessen. Even though they were looking for their graduation dresses, Faye insisted that they check out these fun places and try some of their great food.

R&R enjoyed the spicy rice and beans and loved the hot red sauce they called 'salsa'. The egg rolls in their red sweet and sour sauce from the Chinese street vendor were crispy gooey. Then they had beet borscht from Sam's Deli.

"Seems like we are eating a lot of red stuff today – all of which are different and yet very tasty," Rose commented. "I couldn't begin to tell you which one I like the best. But I will say that red is a popular color for foods from different countries. Why, even spaghetti from old Italy is red!"

"Right, I wonder what Americans eat that is red?" Faye asked.

"Hmm...Since most Americans are from other countries, that would be hard to answer," Ruth pondered. "I imagine that the true American is the Indian, and I don't know what they ate that was red. Do you Rose?"

"Well, all I know is that some of that 'Indian corn' is red."

"Right, the Indian corn has the red in it!" Ruth smiled.

"However, I did learn in my horticulture class that the tomato originated in Mexico," Rose continued. "That's not the United States, but it is close. I guess the Spanish fell in love with that juicy, red orb and, with the potatoes from Peru, they took them both back to Europe; and that, my friends is your history lesson for today!"

"Hey, I know what we eat that is red, and oh so yummy!" Ruth said excitedly. "Red licorice and I see some right there in that store. Let's go get some!" And they all laughed and entered the sweet smelling candy store.

"Alright, Faye, where do we go to get a one-of-a-kind graduation dress?" Ruth asked with her mouth full of that red sweet stuff.

"Ah, so, we turn right at the next corner and we will be at Maxine's. She will make you the most gorgeous dress you can ever imagine!"

"Well, I'm going to ask her to put some Mexican flowers on mine. I've fallen in love with all of the Mexican ladies and their colorful dresses," Rose said taking another bite off her red licorice rope.

The shop was simple with Maxine in the back working on her orders. Her daughter, Vivian, was helping the customers, taking measurements, and advising on styles and choices of fabrics. There was a table to the right with various large books of dress patterns. The three girls veered in that direction while Vivian looked up, gave them a smile and said, "Shopping for a graduation dress, girls?" Vivien - female spelling

"Oh yes, and we've been told that this is the best place in town!" Ruth said as she sat down to look through the catalogue.

Rose joined her while Faye went to the back to see Maxine.

"These are quite nice, Rose, "what do you think of this one?" Rose asked.

"Oh, that would be good for your figure, but not mine. I've got to remember my short waist." Ruth shook her head.

"Well, how about this one?" Ruth suggested.

"Yes, perhaps, but you know what?" Rose looked up and looked into Ruth's eyes. "I don't want a dress that I will only wear once and then pack away. I want something practical that I can travel with, like when I go to Hawaii. I want something simple and easy to pack, not too ruffled and all. Do you know what I mean?"

"Yes, you are right." Ruth agreed, "I am going for the slim and sleek line since I will be traveling to Hawaii with you."

"Do you really think that your parents will allow you to go, just the two of us? I think my parents are going to insist that I find a chaperone," Rose feared. "I don't know who that would be, unless I persuaded my sister, Elizabeth, to go. Frankly, I think the best idea is to persuade my parents that you and I are perfectly capable of chaperoning each other!"

"Oh Rose, you are a caution!" Ruth laughed.

R&R picked out their dresses and surprised Faye by selecting two styles with very simple and sleek lines. They would double as traveling outfits and thus be very practical purchases!

Chapter 8

The day of graduation from Chico High School was warm and slightly breezy. The Dupen family, all that could attend, Uncle Henry, Martha, the eldest Dupen daughter with her students from the Chico Blind School, Mary, the sister who was the editor in New York, Jane, the sister who taught in Siskiyou County, and Elizabeth's family including her husband, Johnny, and her children. Emily, Stephen's wife, arrived from Sacramento with Marian and Emerson in tow both almost in high school, themselves. The Dupen sons, Alfred, Stephen, Adam, and Sam, were overseas still fighting Kaiser Wilhelm and the German soldiers, so they were missed, and also feared for.

The ceremony was in remembrance of the brave soldiers fighting in France as were all of the graduations since 1914 when the war started. But this year's speeches included words like 'termination of this battle for freedom' as most felt that the end was close at hand. And then there was the public reading of all the Chico High School Graduates who had lost their lives in the trenches. Lastly, the returning soldiers sitting in the audience were named and honored. There were tears as well as cheers.

R&R sat together on the outdoor stage next to their 'sister' and 'brother' graduates, wearing the only non-frilly white dresses of the group. They did not mind standing out as they knew that soon these dresses would be packed into their trunks for the lands of Palestine. Not, Hawaii, as they had originally planned, but for Palestine where the Epstein's would join the Cohen's and other doctors and nurses in New York for a journey to the Middle East. They would join the Hadassah group to set up more clinics and administer medical treatment to the poor, ill, and injured. They would treat the Jews as well as the Palestinians; everyone would be welcomed in their clinics.

Hawaii would have to wait, but the girls were not upset about that. Rose knew that any adventure away from Chico was what she wanted. Ruth's heart was with the poor and ill of that desert land; she wanted to help as much as she could. She also thought that seeing the homeland of her people would be a meaningful experience.

They would be gone for the summer and return after the High Holy Days (Rosh Hashanah and Yom Kippur) in September. Ruth would then remain in Sacramento to attend nursing school with Faye, and Rose would stay with her sister-in-law, Emily, until Stephen returned from the war. She would work in the Dupen Jewelry store there and save her money for her trip to Hawaii the following summer. Yes, R&R had it all planned out and meant to follow through on each step.

The only problem was with Rose. She had not told Ruth that her parents had decided last night that they were not going to let her travel to Palestine. After the many meetings with Rachel and Eli Epstein and after much consideration, they felt that with all of their sons fighting in Europe that they could not bear to have one more child overseas. They insisted that she stay home and calm her itchy feet from traveling abroad.

Of course, this did not set well with her at all. She had planned, saved, and expected to be in the Middle East, right in the heart of history being made. She was going to journal her experiences and planned to carry on a correspondence with the local newspaper about her daily experiences. She already had a title for her column: "Follow My Footsteps to Palestine" by Miss Rose Dupen.

Oh, she cried, stomped her feet, and begged for her parents to change their minds but to no avail. By 2 a.m. she finally fell asleep with the resolve that she did not care. She would go anyway and her parents would just have to find out later-when it was too late for her to come back.

Now, this was to be a real adventure. She would sneak out of the house early Monday morning and arrive at Ruth's ready to go. Her parents were leaving tomorrow, Sunday, with Adam's and Sam's families and would be gone for several weeks.

No worries with Mark and his fiancée, as they had postponed their wedding until after his return from France. He was scheduled to enter the army next week. Her parents would just have to understand that no one could stop her when she got a 'bug in her bonnet', so to speak. She was *The Unstoppable Rose Dupen!*

The speeches were over and the graduates stood as their names were read and they advanced across the stage to get their diplomas. R&R followed as they winked at each other and crossed their fingers to show that all was well and that their futures were secure and bright.

Poor Mother and Father, who were sitting in the front row just like they always did when one of their children graduated from the high school, did not know that in just a matter of a few days Mark would be telephoning them with some very disturbing news.

Chapter 9

Monday, May 20th dawned and Rose slipped down the ladder out of her bedroom window. The ladder had remained there since that Black Tuesday in 1905 when downtown Chico had burned. Father thought that the family needed a plan of escape just in case they would ever be caught in a fire again.

This morning there was no fire and Rose was just using the ladder to descend to the back yard and then to quickly get over to Ruth's house. Mark was still asleep. They were to catch the train to Sacramento at 7 a.m. She had already stowed her two suitcases in the garage where the Ford was waiting for Mother and Father's return.

She propped the 'good-bye' note against the sugar bowl on the kitchen table where she knew that Mark would see it; he liked plenty of sugar in his coffee. She bid good-bye to Jackson, the calico kitty, and then with her head held high and her hands grasping the handles of the suitcases, she proudly walked around the corner to embark on a most exciting adventure that she could not possibly fathom. *forsee?*

The parlor light was on at the Epstein's. They were up and finishing their breakfast when Rose knocked on the door. She was ushered in and sat down at the table where they invited her to partake in some potato latkes (pancakes), applesauce, fresh sour cream, and toast with jam.

After packing fruit, boiled eggs, honey cake, and dried fish for their lunch, they loaded into the Dodge coupe with Bernard, their assistant, in the driver's seat. He was going to drop them at the train station and then return the car for the duration of the summer. The Epstein Clinic would be closed until October with Bernard merely maintaining the grounds and dealing with the mail. Dr. Fulbright would once again be the only doctor on call in Chico.

"I was disappointed that I did not have a chance to speak with your mother after the graduation Saturday," Mrs. Epstein addressed Rose, "I wanted to wish them a good trip and, also, to go over a few details about our itinerary. The mail will be slow from the Middle East, so I wanted to let her know about that. We essentially will be out of contact for a while, but for her not to worry."

"Oh, Mother was surrounded by all the family and grandchildren and was up to her elbows in runny noses and skinned knees. They left yesterday with Adam and Sam's families so they would not have to travel alone. Evidently the trip down for the graduation was quite an adventure, so I heard from my two sisters-in-law, AnnaBeth and BethAnne. Mark and I were pretty much forgotten and were soon sent on our way to the Graduation Dance. When I awoke on Sunday morning, they had already left. I spent the day packing and cleaning the house. Mark went with Bertha's family on a picnic, so it was just me and the kitty, Jackson, at the old Dupen house! I liked the quiet, I must admit!"

"Well, ok. Just as long as your parents know and understand our trip schedule."

"Oh, yes, they have that posted in the kitchen and even got out the old atlas to see exactly where we will be."

In reality, Rose had been instructed to let the Epstein's know that she *would not* be accompanying them on this excursion to Palestine. In fact, she had insisted that she tell them herself as she knew that Ruth would be horribly disappointed and wanted to comfort her. She told her parents that she wanted to pick 'just the right moment'. That all worked well, and now she was left with more lies to tell to the Epsteins. She just hoped that she could keep them all straight.

Rachel Epstein had made sure that she gave Rose's parents the phone number of the head offices for Hadassah. They would know all the information about the convoy of doctors and nurses traveling to Jerusalem. Messages could certainly be conveyed through them. Rose had decided that this information would not be good for her parents to have after they found out that she had stowed away against their orders, so she took that piece of paper and tore it up. *I think I've covered my trail pretty well. I have my money safe in my suitcase and satchel, so I'm not worried about being penniless. It was great that most everyone gave me money gifts for graduation. Little did they know that I would be using it on my little jaunt to a foreign country!*

Chapter 10

On the train to New York, they studied Hebrew and Arabic so that they would have some idea of how to communicate while in Jerusalem. Dr. Epstein, Eli, had brought along primers and held classes with both families twice a day for one hour and then assigned homework as well. Rose was not anticipating 'school' on the trip, but knew that any reason that she would try to get herself out of the lessons would most certainly fail. Besides, better to be prepared to enter a world of different languages than run the risk of getting lost and misunderstood.

After a while the girls were conversing as if it was a fun code in which to keep secrets from their parents. The parents were not so quick to pick up the new vocabulary and were being repeatedly put in the middle of funny capers that were designed by the girls.

They now knew how to ask for a drink, order a sandwich, talk on the telephone, and could identify the words for 'store', 'hotel', 'car', 'horse', and 'cafe' plus at least a hundred more. Their confidence was soaring until Eli insisted somewhere in the vicinity of Iowa that they needed to learn the words for medical terminology. Since they would be working in medical clinics, it was important for them to be able to communicate with the patients. It was true that Palestine was part of the British Commonwealth and that the government agencies used English as their official language, but the common person, who was either Arabian or Jewish, could only speak the native language of their region.

Ruth and Faye took their lessons seriously. They knew how important it would be to aid those by being able to communicate easily. They fully intended to work extra hard.

Rose, on the other hand, could not get on board with all of the medical vocabulary. She was picturing herself conversing with the natives about their homes, families, dreams and hopes. She knew that she would be assisting the other nurses, but did not really see herself doing the actual 'nursing' duties. Consequently, her efforts to learn the medical terms were lax and somewhat resented. *Why should I have to learn that stuff when I truly do not want to be a nurse? I'll be happy just to hand them the bandages and iodine that they need. Besides, maybe I can work in the kitchens. I'm real good at making bread, fried chicken, cole slaw, and chicken noodle soup. I'll do that.*

What Rose did not truly understand was that all able bodies would be required to help with the medical cases, regardless of whether they wanted to or not. There would not be much need for a cook to make dishes that were not familias? common in Jerusalem, and more than likely, she would be taking lessons from the local women on how to make hummus, falafel, flat breads, and tabbouleh.

By now, Rose figured that the whole family had been informed that she had run away with Ruth's family to Jerusalem. She would send them a letter from New York before leaving on the ocean liner and after they arrived in Liverpool, England, their first port, she would tell the Epstein's of her caper. By then they would be stuck with her and they would have to make the best of it. She was confident that all would end well. It just had to. This was going to be the best experience of her life.

Mark could not believe his eyes. What was he reading? Was this a joke? Rose couldn't have been so selfish and unthinking to have really taken off with the Epsteins, could she?

Well, if any Dupen would do it, probably Rose would be the one. Mother always called her 'the one Dupen child with the stiff neck'; "There's just no telling what she will do next once she gets a bug in her bonnet," Mother would say. Father simply would smile at her strong will with a twinkle in his eye and say that it was amazing how such a pretty girl could be as stubborn as he was in his teens. Mother would then look at him with disgust and walk out of the room.

Of course, Rose gave no thought to the fact that now Mark, her twin brother, would have to pick up the pieces of the mess she had left behind and call Mother and Father in Montana, inform Elizabeth and Martha in Chico and then let Emily in Sacramento and Judith in Los Angeles know what was the latest drama Rose had spun for the family to cope with.

This was a big one, for sure. She did not merely hop a train to San Francisco on a lark for some fun with girlfriends. Oh no...She was heading to a dangerous spot half way around the globe. And why... just to see something different because she was bored with Chico? Does she ever think of anyone else besides herself? *Adventure; she's always talking like all she wants in her life is more adventure.* Mark thought. *Well this adventure could just about do her in, I'm afraid. Mother and Father might send her to a convent as her punishment. But she'd probably find some way to escape that, knowing her. Yep, knowing her, my sister would certainly figure a way out.*

While rubbing his brow, Mark reread the note that Rose had left behind:

Mark,

You won't find me in my room, or over at Elizabeth's. In fact, I am no longer in Chico. I could simply not miss going to Palestine; truly the most incredible opportunity to see another world. Besides, the war is ending soon and I am confident that all is well. I really think I can be of some help over there. Anyway, what's done is done.

*I am sorry that you have to tell everyone, but it is the only
way I could possibly have done this. Besides, what are twins
for? I will send postcards when I can, certainly from New
York.*
As ever,
Your sister, Rose
P.S. I owe you, brother!

"Yeah, what are twins for?" Mark said aloud. "It
certainly is not a two-way street in this family. I seem to be
doing all the rescuing of Rose. Rarely, do I need rescuing, so I
guess I am the sane one and will be constantly in this position
of being the arbitrator between her and the parents. Well, this
time I'm not doing it. I'm simply going to mail this note to
them in Reno and let them to do as they wish."

With that said, he looked for an envelope. While
scrounging through the desk, he realized that sending this
note to Mother and Father would accomplish nothing. It
would be best to tell the Chico family and together they could
come up with a plan. Yes, he would tell Bertha first. She
would have a good idea, Mark was sure.

Chapter 11

Bertha agreed that Mark needed to stop rescuing Rose from her various antics. Yes, she would come to the house later and put together a meal. They were formally engaged now, so offering to prepare something during this time of upset for her fiancée's family would be a nice gesture. They called the two remaining siblings in Chico and Uncle Henry. Since today was Sunday, the dinner would be early, at 3 p.m.

"Thank you so much, dearest one," Mark held her hand, "for doing this for me. I would rather have you with me when I read Rose's note and then the others can decide what to do with my crazy sister's latest caper."

"Of course, my fiancée," Bertha smiled. "Soon this will be my official family and I think something as wild as Rose running off to Palestine deserves the family to all decide what to do about telling your mother and father. Undoubtedly, news like this would ruin their stay with the grandchildren and they may even wish to return home immediately. However, I don't think there is much they can do now. What's done is done."

Their conversation was interrupted by the ring of the telephone. It was Elizabeth returning Mark's call. Soon, all of this would be over and this event would be added to the Dupen Family Chronicles of Adventures and Capers.

The dishes were done and all were settled in the parlor for their coffees and cigars. Uncle Henry loved his Havana's and usually brought enough for the other men in the family. Even Mark was entertaining one as he settled into the green velvet side chair. He had just finished reading Rose's note and was waiting for someone to have a reaction, make a comment, or at least breathe.

"You mean Father and Mother specifically told Rose that she could not accompany the Epstein's on this trip, and she ran away anyway?" Johnny asked puzzled. "I don't get it. Why would she do that?"

"We all know Rose and her strong will. Remember how she threw her tantrums when Mother tried to wash her hair," Elizabeth added. "Nothing's really changed. She is an adult now, and is still minding her own wants and needs first. Actually, I cannot say that I am too surprised. I knew that she was very excited about this trip. Mother and Father's second thoughts about her going are understandable to me, but certainly not to Rose."

"I guess it does not help that I am off to France in a few days." Mark responded. "They have too many of their children in the war, and allowing Rose to travel to another hot spot in the world pushed them over the edge, I fear. My problem," he continued, "is that I do not want to be the sole person handling this. I think we should all decide what to do. It is too big of a problem for me to handle alone."

"I agree," Uncle Henry said while puffing on his cigar. "Well, did she think that she might not have a family to come back to if she keeps up with these shenanigans? Obviously not; hmmm, I'm inclined to allow Cate and Patrick to have their visit with the families without telling them, but knowing Cate, she would skin me alive if we did not tell them right now. In fact, she will be angry that we waited this long."

"Mark, you had better ring them up at Sam's house. They always stay there," Martha, the oldest Dupen sibling announced. "Let's get this nasty chore over with."

"All right, then, who is going to call them," Mark asked.

"Well, the note is addressed to you, so you had better do it," Bertha answered. "We'll all stand by so we can offer support if you need it."

They gathered around the telephone in the great mahogany hallway. Mark spoke to the operator and she said that she would put the call through and then call them back when she got Mother and Father on the line. They all waited. They did not talk. One could only hear the sipping of coffee and the puffing of cigars. Really, there was not much to say.

Chapter 12

Mark reported to duty; it was a tearful parting from Bertha, but basically she had been prepared. Mother and Father realized that there was nothing that they could do from neither Reno nor Chico in getting Rose back where she belonged, so they remained with their grandchildren. Mother was just sick about it, though. Both of the twins would be gone when she returned to that big empty Dupen house. Father knew and understood Rose's spirit and remembered with a chuckle when he set out for America from England with hardly a farewell to his parents. He had a mission to accomplish; to track down that scoundrel of a brother. Both he and Henry would find him and take back the money that was owed them. Yes, he was after the inheritance, but most importantly he was excited about the voyage to a new world with his new bride, Cate. So, he did understand Rose's wanderlust.

Mark boarded the train for Sacramento and then the trans-continental that would deposit him in New York. From there he would board a liner for England. Finally, he would be transported to France. There would be a brief training on surviving the life in the French trenches and then on to the front he would go. Handling a rifle was nothing new to him as he had hunted extensively with Father and his four older brothers.

He would be issued his uniform in Sacramento and then travel the rest of the way with his unit. The army life would be his new world. His buddies from high school would be with him and together they would land in France and be the final force to defeat the Kaiser.

They were a tough bunch of kids, having been great football and baseball players. They would show the Germans how to win a war! He knew that all the girls loved men in uniform, so Mark was looking forward to sending a picture home to Bertha with him in his full regalia. She would place it on her bureau and greet him every morning. Then, when he returned and all was put to rest in Europe, they would marry, he in his handsome uniform and she in a lovely lace dress sewn by her wonderfully talented hands. It was going to be perfect, he just knew it.

His unit had just arrived at The Times Square Railroad Station and was told to wait there until the troop buses arrived and gathered them up. They would be transported to the troop ship that was loading soldiers, supplies and a small group of medical personnel heading to Jerusalem. Evidently this group was part of a Zionist movement that was bringing sorely needed medical help to the stricken areas of the Middle East that were experiencing rampant diseases and poverty.

All Mark knew was that he was finally heading over to Europe and would be in the trenches with the other allies pulverizing those Germans. It felt good to have a purpose. The need to free Europe from the Ottomans and subsequently the Germans meant that perhaps once and for all ruthless dictators would have no place in the world.

It is true that the United States did not enter the war officially until the sinking of seven merchant ships by the German U-boats. These were the undersea boats patrolling the North Atlantic with the purpose of cutting off the flow of supplies to England. President Woodrow Wilson had already warned Germany against the sinking of any more passenger ships like the British Lusitania in 1915, but they continued to sink any merchant or troop ships navigating the Atlantic shipping lanes.

Finally, the British military intercepted a telegram sent by Germany to Mexico asking them to enter the war on their side with the promise that they (Germany) would help Mexico to recover their old territories lost in the Spanish-American War. That would mean that Germany would help Mexico to get back the states of: Texas, Arizona and New Mexico.

President Wilson, quite alarmed, declared war on Germany April 6, 1917. Daily, ships of troops left New York harbor for the trenches in France. By 1918, 10,000 American soldiers were arriving on French soil every day. It was here that they were quickly trained and then shoved over to the Western Front for trench warfare.

Mark knew all of this, but was confident that the war was nearing its end, and then he would have the victory under his belt in no time. He did not anticipate having to stay in the trenches for too long. He would become an American fighting machine with his new rifle and bayonet that would be issued to him prior to his sailing. He would treat his 'sweet Betsy' with love, and nightly keep her polished and oiled. He would be the best soldier ever, he often said to himself.

Chapter 13

Broadway, New York, was not happy or brightly lit the second week of June, 1918. Fourteen months previously, President Woodrow Wilson asked Congress for a declaration of war. Now twenty-five American divisions were already in France, and fresh ones were leaving weekly.

The group of Hadassah doctors and nurses who gathered on 42nd Street in the early evening of June 11 were making an effort to be happy and carefree their last day on home soil. At midnight they would report at the pier for duty overseas. Most of the group wanted their last meal in America to be something quite memorable. Some suggested a big steak, others wanted prime rib. Regardless, they all stayed together and feasted on beef and then headed to Coney Island to have their fortunes told. What better time than today to find out what this new adventure would bring them.

Rose, Faye and Ruth were excited to be on Coney Island, to ride the carousel, and feast on hot pretzels and cotton candy. They marveled at the sights and loved the circus-like atmosphere.

"I love being here," Rose exclaimed. "It reminds me of our October Carnival back home. Don't you agree, Ruth?" "Oh definitely," Ruth responded "I just miss your mother's apple pie that she is so famous for."

"Yes, she's won many blue ribbons with that recipe," Rose added. "And she still won't share it with us girls! We'll probably get it when she is on her deathbed when she knows that she will not be able to make it herself anymore…ha-ha!"

"Oh look, cotton candy, girls," Faye pointed out. "Let's go and get some. I'm sure we won't find any of that in Palestine. I love that stuff."

"Well, I'm saving my pennies for some homemade taffy," Rose said.

"Oh yes, Rose," Ruth swooned. "And my favorite is the salt-water taffy. It's just heavenly."

"Oh, speaking of salt water, girls," Faye changed the subject. "Did you know that there is a place in Palestine that is called 'The Dead Sea'? Nothing grows in it because it is salt water. Imagine, an inland sea that is so salty that you just can't sink."

"Oh, that must be like the Great Salt Lake in Utah, Faye," Rose offered.

"Oh, I forgot about our own 'Dead Sea' here in the United States. Anyway, when you mentioned salt-water taffy, it just reminded me that we might get to see the Dead Sea that I have read about."

"I imagine that we will see so many places that we have only read about and that will amaze us," Rose added.

"I'm sure that I will not believe that I will be in the presence of the great Wailing Wall right in Jerusalem," Ruth commented. "Have you heard of that wall, Rose?"

"Why yes, I think you told me once that it was the last remaining wall of the original Jewish Temple from King Solomon, right? At least that is what I remember you saying."
"Very good, Rose," Ruth laughed. "You get an 'A+' today in history!"

"Come, girls," Faye urged. "This is the Hall of Mirrors. It is so funny; they have all kinds that can make you look totally misshapen...you know, tall, fat, skinny!"

"Oh, they have one of those in San Francisco at the beach play land," Rose answered. "And I dare say that I did not look very pretty in any of them. I'm not sure I want to see my ugly self in any of those again!"

"Oh come on, Rose," Ruth countered. "It will be fun and silly. We need to be as silly as we can because after tonight, I think that life for us will become very serious."

"Do any of you think about what it's going to be like in Palestine?" Faye asked.

"Oh it doesn't matter to me," Rose giggled. "I just love an adventure in any shape or form."

"Well, I do too," Faye returned. "But this excursion could be a lot more shocking than we might have ever imagined. I overheard some of the nurses talking about how they had heard reports about the terrible conditions in Jerusalem. Besides the wounded soldiers to treat, there are also a lot of the villagers who are suffering from disease and starvation. I think we will find these poor people needing any help that we can give them, even if it is just a drink of water."

"Oh I'm not worried about that stuff," Rose boldly stated. "I'm so excited about traveling abroad, that I don't care what I will encounter. Just the adventure of going makes all of that worth it."

"As for me," Ruth piped up. "I'm only going to think about being here now on Coney Island and I'm going to get the most out of the next few hours we have here before we board the ship."

"Yeah, me too!"

"I agree."

"See you in the Hall of Mirrors!"

"After that, let's go to the giant indoor slide. Now that looks like a lot of fun!"

"Yes," Rose added. "Let's make the next two hours the best ever!"

"I just hope that I don't get too sea sick," Ruth worried.

"Oh, don't worry about that," Faye laughed. "We'll just put you on the roller coaster tonight and that will toughen up your stomach!"

"Oh no!" Ruth laughed. "I'll surely get sick on that!"

Chapter 14

They had gathered at the pier at midnight and by the time they were loaded, found their berths, and nestled into the sounds of this troop ship, they then realized that there would be no turning back.

Rose knew that the next few months would be sealed for her either on a ship, on a train chugging through the desert, or emerged in the medical needs of the Palestinian people. She realized that she would be with the British, the Arabs, and the Jews and she was learning what it meant to be a Zionist and that the Jews were desperately trying to claim this small piece of land wedged between mighty Arab countries for themselves.

Jews were arriving in droves from various other parts of the world, namely Russia, Poland, Hungary, Germany, Italy and France. Despite the dangers of being caught in the crossfire of the mighty war currently raging, mostly in France and North Africa, immigrants were arriving in a steady flow. It seemed that the populations of the world were constantly moving either in and out of war or in search of safer places for their families and their beliefs.

It was now common knowledge that almost a year ago the British had put forth the *Balfour Declaration* which promised a Jewish National Home in Palestine. Now those Jews wanting to establish and be part of the rebuilding of Jerusalem for all of the Jewish people could enter this land of *milk and honey* without hesitation.

However, there was no land of *milk and honey* yet. The Arab government was livid with this turn of events and began arresting Jews, limiting their travels, and razing their homes. Finally, through the course of the war, the British marched against them and defeated the Arab army. In Jerusalem, in December of 1917, a peace agreement was signed between General Allenby of England and the Arab Sultan. Now the Jews were free to settle in their own territory with the military support of their benefactors, the British military.

The land was dry and not welcoming to the many ship loads of Jews arriving weekly. Starvation, typhus and complications from trachoma (disease of the eyes), and the over population of fleas led to medical conditions that were, at times, insurmountable.

There had been little funding and few personnel to equip the Jewish hospitals of the area. The need for money, supplies and medical doctors and their nurses were multiplying daily.

Henrietta Szold knew this and had approached her Zionist Women's Organization for support. Their fund drives to support the Jewish Medical Centers in Palestine were fueled by the atrocious reports from the area describing deplorable conditions for the children as well as pregnant and nursing mothers. Their sympathies were piqued and it was Szold's organization, later known as *Hadassah,* which supported the deployment of Rose's fellow travelers to this infested area in the Middle East.

She lay on her narrow bed that she shared with Ruth, gazing up at the ceiling of somewhat rusted metal pondering this new found information about a part of the world that scarcely anyone in Chico cared about.

Along with their daily language lessons, they were required to participate in history lessons presented by Faye's parents. Now this she found interesting as she had always wanted to be on the cutting edge of every hot spot in the world. *I predict that Palestine and the surrounding countries will keep the interest of everyone for a long time. The Jews want their homeland back and I'm sure that the Arabs are not too pleased about giving up even one inch of it to them,* she thought.

The lilting of the ship as it moved out of the harbor soon put these young women to sleep. It was the next morning that the effects of the sea-sickness would wreak havoc upon these tender passengers.

The storm had hit suddenly by 4 a.m. and before the Cohen's and Epstein's knew it, they were up and clamoring either to the toilet or over the balusters on deck. The crew told the passengers that all they needed was their 'sea legs' to take over and they were going to be fine.

Ruth turned absolutely grey, Faye was not to be seen for the rest of the day, and Rose decided that it was simply a case of mind over matter. If she did not *mind* the natural motions upon the sea, then it just would not *matter* to her. She focused on the library aboard and buried her nose and eyes into all the history of the region surrounding Palestine that she could get her hands on. Oh, once or twice she felt a few acrobats in her stomach, but she merely squared her chin, and demanded her own way over her queasiness. She did not have time to be sick and would simply not allow the thought to enter her being.

Next, she tried to get Faye and Ruth to explore the different levels of the ship with her but their insistence on being incapacitated left them unable to rise from their beds. So, Ruth took off by herself.

Of course, she knew the path between their small cabin and the dining room very well but she wanted to see what was beyond that. There were military troops aboard, but nowhere did she see them. Not even one. Oh, they were there alright as she often heard the crew referring to the new *doughboys* on the upper deck performing their duties of swabbing, repairing ropes, and checking their weapons and ammo.

Rose knew that she was not allowed up there on the military deck but that did not stop her from wanting to find a way up there to spy on them. A young boy in uniform was certainly a delight to see at any time. Since Ruth and Faye would not accompany her on this adventure, she would just have to play Kit Carson by herself and go exploring.

Chapter 15

She had found a good spot in which to hide; she wedged between some boxes under the stairwell leading up to the top deck. She was in a perfect place to hear the conversations as the soldiers went up and down the stairs. For the most part, the boys were trying to get through each hour without losing their last meal. Most of them had never been on a ship before and were eager to get over to France to show the Kaiser a thing or two. Some expressed the loneliness they felt already for their families and the girls they had left behind.

Rose was glad that she had packed a pair of her brother's pants and a shirt. She had a suspicion that there might be times when she would not want to be seen in a dress and this was one of those times. How could she possibly hide close enough to the men wearing a dress? No, she had to act and look like a boy. She'd often worn a pair of Mark's pants at home although she caught heck from the parents and Mark. They could not understand that a dress was just impractical sometimes. *Try climbing a tree in a dress*, she would say back to them; and they would just say that a girl has no business being up in a tree. *Pshaw! I say. I'll sit in a tree and read a book any day and no one is going to stop me!*

And here she was in Mark's knickers with one of his hats on ready to make her debut and climb up the stairs to the top deck. *Best to go up when no one is coming down,* she thought. She wanted to put some dirt on her face so that no one would notice her fine features. She rubbed her hand on the planks below her boots and scrubbed it into her face. Ah dirt...such an earthy smell. Days of playing in the backyard mud puddles ran through her mind. *Those were wonderful moments feeling the wet dirt ooze up between my toes.*

The stairway finally seemed to be empty of human boots so she ventured out of her hidden niche and boldly hoisted herself up to the first step. *Now don't be afraid, Miss Rose. Remember how Mother always says that you have enough gumption for 5. Keep your eyes down and just take the stairs like you own them!* And that is just what she did. Counting each one as she emerged on deck, she ended with 13...*uh oh...now that's bad luck!* And she allowed herself a little giggle. *My voice...I've got to change my voice so I do not sound like a girl. Hmmm...'Now that is bad luck'* she said out loud in a lower register. *That's just going to have to do for now. I don't plan on speaking anyhow.*

She took a quick look around and saw a rather wide pole that perhaps she could hide behind. She firmly but quickly strode over to it and assumed a position of keeping watch over something. Over what, she was not too sure. She spied a bucket with a scrub brush in it and bent down to the planking to act like she was scrubbing the deck. *This should work for a while,* she thought. *As I scrub I'll just slowly move myself around so I can get a better view.*

Before she knew it, there were two large boots standing in front of her. She heard a voice, evidently belonging to the boots. "Psst, what are you doing here, mate?"

"Uh, just doin' my job; cook caught me sneaking a biscuit so he sent me up here to do my penitence," she fabricated.

"Can't say as I blame ya, kid; *Cookie* is one of the best. Hey, ain't seen ya before; where ya been hidin' yourself?"

"Um, nowhere; just busy in the kitchen is all. Wish I could join you on the battlefield. I'd show them Krauts a thing or two."

"Well, you could join, you know," the boots said. "You look pretty young, but I'm only 17 and they took me. What are you; 15 or 16?"

"Ya, my parents are dead and I had nowhere to go and I didn't wanna be put in some orphanage. I came aboard this ship and hid in the kitchen pantry. Everything was good until the cook's brother found me. But I was lucky. He said they needed more help, so here I am. Guess I'll just stay put and fight the war here by cookin' you doughboys some good vittles."

"That is if you don't eat them all yourself! Say, what's yer name, mate?" boots asked.

"Uh, they call me Robin cuz I can whistle real good. I whistle in the kitchen a lot. Yeah, and I won't eat no vittles of yours. You need your strength so you can push them Jerries back."

"Well, it's been real nice meetin' you Robin. I'll be listening for your whistling when I'm in the mess eatin' your fine rations! By the by, my name's Jimmy; yep, Jimmy Morrison. Be seein' ya!"

"Yeah, likewise, I'm sure."

After the boots left, Rose took a big sigh and silently gave herself a pat on the back for creating such an interesting character as Robin. Hmm, she would need a last name. *How about...Smith; no, that's just plain boring. Something with a 'D' so I can have the same initials that I have now... Davis? Yeah, that sounds good. Robin Davis. And, I guess I am 15 years old. Funny how I just became 3 years younger in no time at all!*

Chapter 16

"Yes, and there I was having this conversation with this real-live soldier! Can you believe that? Just pinch me and I will tell you the story again!" Rose was beside herself with glee.

"Gosh, Rose, you really do have some nerve!" Faye whispered.

"Oh, she does this crazy stuff all the time. That's why I just love her to death!" Ruth said, giving her a big hug. "Yep, Rose is the wild one and I just follow along for the fun!"

"And, you know what? This fella, Jimmy, he's real nice and I want to get to know him. I'm going back up there tomorrow. I want to find out where he's from and all. He might even introduce me to some of the other boys in his unit. That would be exciting, don't you think?"

"But Rose," Faye said in alarm. "What if they realize that you are an imposter? You might have to walk the plank!" And then the three girls burst out laughing and acted like they were walking the plank to their deaths.

The next day Rose (or Robin), met Jimmy up on deck after the noon meal. She had to admit that all of a sudden this boring trip to the other side of the world was becoming more exciting now that she had created for herself a new character. Once again, she was thankful for Mark's clothing as she pulled his jacket tightly around her neck to fight off the sudden chill of being out on the open deck.

"Hey, Robin, whatcha doin' up here today? Cookie still mad at ya?" Jimmy squatted down next to her.

She moved off to the side a little. "Nah, just hopin' I'd get to see ya again. Wanted to know where you're from and all. Maybe see some other soldiers. I just think you're real brave, and all. You know, and all."

"Yeah, I get it. You wish you could be going with us; Can't blame ya. No I can't. Well, I hail from Ohio, little town next to Cincinnati. Ever been to Ohio, little guy?"

Rose shook her head 'no'. "Ain't ever been outside of New York. No reason to, I guess. What's it like in Ohio?"

"Nice, real nice. Prettiest sunsets you ever did see, and I'm tellin' you the truth."

"Did some of your mates sign up with you? Are they here now?"

"Well, yes, as a matter of fact, ol' Percy come with me. Besides killin' them Germans, he wanted to meet some of those real pretty French girls! Oh heck, I guess that is part of why I wanted to sign up too!" Jimmy laughed. "Ya wanna meet Percy?"

"I suppose. Don't bother me none."

"Well, c'mon then. They're down in the mess playin' Checkers. You good at Checkers? We're havin' a tournament. So far, no one's beat this one fella. We call him *Cali* for short cuz he's from California. But Percy's gone against him cuz he's got the talent. He can beat everyone I know of at Checkers. But I don't know about Cali. I've never seen anyone win like he does. You'd almost think he's cheatin', 'cept it's pretty hard to cheat at checkers, doncha know!"

So, Rose followed Jimmy down the ladder to the mess. *Oh boy, I've really done it now,* she chastised herself. *For sure, I'm going to get caught. I gotta get more dirt on my face and hands. I just look too dainty and that is not good!*
They entered the dinner hall and Jimmy led her over to a group of boys gathered around two players hoping to win the Checkers tournament.

"Ho-ho Percy, that's a good move," a voice piped up.

"John, you almost got him," said another.

"Alright, alright, let me think," John ordered.

"Oh my Lord, did ya hear that? He says he's gotta think! What's the world comin' to?" answered one of Percy's rooters.

"Well, it don't matter who wins cuz I'm better than both of ya, that's a sure bet!"

"Oh quiet, Tiny, you ain't gonna win no tournament. Don't worry Percy, he's just joshin' ya."

Rose peeked over someone's shoulder to see this 'Tiny' fellow. Surprise, surprise, he wasn't tiny at all. She could scarcely keep her giggle inside. Tiny was as big as an elephant! Well, not that big, but maybe a baby one for sure. Jimmy motioned her to come over by him. He pushed her ahead of him since she was shorter. She was glad that she hadn't put on any rose water this morning or that sweet smell would have been a dead giveaway that she was not a boy.

She peered over someone's shoulder and saw the two players. The Checker board was nearly empty with 3 kings remaining for each man. Indeed, this was a close match. She knew about close matches as she and Mark were hailed as Checker champions at their high school. Mark was the boys' champion and Rose was the girls'. There was talk that it was all a Dupen family conspiracy but the duo had won their titles fair and square. She figured that if she had the chair belonging to Percy that she could take John in 3 or 4 moves. She wished that she could have been part of this tournament. As much as she loved Checkers, she also knew that any more exposure than absolutely necessary would give rise to someone finding out her true identity. *Better to be patient and play it safe*, she said to herself.

For a while Rose actually felt like Robin Davis the kitchen stowaway and figured she was blending in nicely with the others.

"So Robin, what do you think?" Jimmy asked. "Will Percy win? He's everyone's favorite."

"Hard to say but I think he could if he concentrated. The next move will be crucial," Rose answered.

Before they knew it, there was a loud wallop and Percy's fans were jumping up and down and shaking his shoulders with a victorious fervor.

"You did it! You did it!" they yelled.

John solemnly rose from the table and extended his hand for the congratulatory handshake. "Good luck against Cali, Percy. He's a tough one to beat. I haven't won a game off of him yet!" he said.

Percy sat back down to clear the board and prepare for the final match. Rose wanted to see this so she decided to hang tight and push her luck just a little bit more. A spot opened up right behind Percy so she scooted over there. Now she could clearly see both of their strategies. She couldn't help it but she was getting excited almost as if she was the one going up against this Cali-guy. *Percy has good potential and just might prove to be the champ. I like the way he won't be rushed and contemplates each move to its fullest. That shows that he is thinking at least 2 or 3 moves ahead.*

"Say, where *is* Cali? Someone go get 'im," Jimmy yelled out. Tiny made his way out of the middle of the crowd and went into another room.

"Hey, Cali," he summoned, "you're up. Percy took John, now come show us your stuff."

A tall lanky kid came through the doorway, somewhat shuffling toward the crowd. Both hands were shoved into his pockets. He kept his eyes to the ground as he moved closer and assumed his place at the table.

He certainly did not look like a champion. He actually looked somewhat shy and withdrawn. They made way for him and he sat down opposite Percy, and Rose's eyes grew large and her mouth dropped open. The first thing he did was to wipe the back of his left hand across his nose, scratch his right ear with the same hand and then clasp both hands with fingers laced together and flex them outward so that everyone could hear his knuckles crack. *There's only one person who does that before playing a game of Checkers and I know who it is! Oh my goodness!*

Chapter 17

What was the likelihood of this happening? Rose was in a state of shock because sitting opposite Percy was her twin brother, Mark Dupen. Yes, it was true. There he was in the flesh wearing his army issued clothes; a white undershirt and green dungarees. Around his neck was a chain with a tag on it. It more than likely had his name on it with his ID numbers.

Well go figure, Rose said to herself, *what a strange turn of events. Imagine my twin and I are on our way to the Great War. Drat, I hope he doesn't look up. My luck and he would notice me for sure. I'll just edge behind this fella here. I can still see the moves but I am not so conspicuous. I just gotta see Mark or Cali as he is called now, defeat Percy royally. I know he will. No one has ever defeated Mark. Or me, for that matter! What would be really funny is if I challenged ol' Cali here to a match of our own. The thing is we can never defeat one another. First he wins, then I win, it's always a tie; sometimes we stalemate, but most of the time not. Our matches are truly spectacular! I am just so tempted to do it...but, better not. I really do not want to blow my cover. I might need this boy-disguise for a while longer.*

From the very beginning it was not hard to see that Percy was fighting for his life, so to speak. Cali double and triple jumped his men, and he was thus left with very few in which to turn into kings. The game lasted a mere 10 minutes and the hall exploded with cheers for Cali. He casually stood up from the table, shook Percy's hand and then turned and quietly and shyly slipped out of the room.

Poor Percy was left in shock. Rose, on the other hand, was patting herself on the back because she called the match in favor of Mark. A 10 minute game for Mark was not unusual. He didn't like to dance around his opponent. He just dove in and brought on the victory as fast as he could. Besides, she knew that shy Mark was not fond of being a spectacle in front of a crowd. He wanted it over with as quickly as possible. And it was, too, over in a flash.

The boys remaining were still laughing and patting each other on their backs and yelling about how Cali had really shown Percy and all of his fans. They were proud that they had stood by him, the silent but deadly victor. In a way, it was what they thought fighting the war in France was going to be like. They would sweep the Germans and Turks out in one offensive move and before everyone realized what had hit them, the United States would claim the victory that would end the war. They were sure of it and planned to be home before Christmas.

Before Rose could think she uttered out loud, "I bet I coulda beat that guy in even less time than he beat Percy."

"What are ya sayin' little fella?" asked Jimmy.

Rose looked up at him and realized that she had just let slip out of her mouth the very words she was trying to keep a secret. "Uh, what?"

"You just said that you could beat Cali." Jimmy said.

"Ok. Yeah. I suppose I could," she said in a whisper. "But I didn't want anyone to hear that. Jus' sayin' is all."

"Well, you either mean it or not. Which is it?" Jimmy grabbed Rose's shoulder.

"Yeah, I'm the champ back home in my neighborhood. I could beat him."

What was she saying? What had she just done? There she goes again, heading out into unchartered territory where she will probably end up in big trouble. *Sometimes I just can't help myself. I just love adventure and anything that gets my heart beating loudly. Risky actions always bring exciting times and lots of attention and don't I love that! Well, here I go again.*

"Hey fellas, wait just a minute," Jimmy yelled out. "This little guy here says that he can beat ol' Cali. Better call him back. We got a challenge going on. Anyone want to make a wager? I bet that Robin can beat our champ, Cali. What do ya say?"

Tiny went after Cali while the rest of the boys laid down their bets. Rose pulled her hat down even further on her head. She had to keep her identity a secret from Mark or the whole caper would be ruined. She would beat him, she just knew she could since he had been playing for a while now and was starting to get tired. This would be her first match and she was sharp as a tack. Besides, she knew her brother and she had seen the weariness enter his eyes while playing Percy. She went over and sat in the seat that Percy had occupied. It wasn't exactly a good luck seat, but it would do. Within minutes Mark came into the room and sauntered over to the chair opposite her.

So far so good, she said to herself. *He hasn't even looked at me yet.*

"Hey Cali," Jimmy said. "Check out this kid over here. He says that he can beat ya, no sweat! What do ya think of that?"

One of Cali's mates yelled out, "Ain't nobody gonna beat our Cali from Cal-ee-for-nee-ay, right Cali?"

"We'll see 'bout that," Mark said in his soft voice. He wasn't going to make a spectacle of himself so he kept his head down so as not to make eye contact with his opponent. As he addressed the board with his usual ritual of wiping his nose with his left hand etc., he whispered to his challenger, "go ahead, you go first, kid."

Rose made her usual first move, Mark countered as he always did when playing her and the rest of the game went just as she expected until the final few moves when she had a choice of giving over the game to him and not risk being discovered as a girl *or*, not.

Rose really wanted to be the victor. She wanted to outshine her brother and what better way to do it than to beat him at his own best game in front of his shipmates. But would that be fair to him? What would the rest of his days be like for him? Did she want to strip him of this small glory? Who knows? He was not merely going to summer camp with these boys; he was heading off to war. What if he is killed and the last memory she would have of her twin was of the embarrassment he felt when he lost the championship to her, his sister who had made fools of them all by sneaking into the soldier's quarters.

For once, Rose began to think about what her actions could do to someone else. Mother and Father had tried to teach her that her actions are not just for her, but also for the others for whom she would affect. *I guess this is what they meant. I'm having a vision of what my victory would mean to dear old Mark. I would just die if he didn't come back from the war and this was the last memory I had of him...him being humiliated. Nope, I just can't do it. Yes, this is really me talking. I guess I just love him too much to do that to him. Darn! And I really wanted to show him up.*

After the game, Mark stood and reached across the table. Rose outstretched her hand to shake his and realized that she had forgotten to take off her ring. Quickly she put her hand in her pocket, but not before Mark's expression changed on his face. He couldn't really see her face, but he recognized the shirt she was wearing since it was from his wardrobe back home. He pulled his hand back and merely said, "Good game, kid, I almost thought you had me a couple-a moves back. Say, what's your name?"

"Uh, Robin, sir; Uh, Robin Davis; I come from right here in New York. Sure wish I could come along and fight them Krauts with ya, sir. Ya play a good game, sir. Yes, thought I was to win also. Good luck and all." And Rose turned and headed out of the hall as quickly as possible. How could she have forgotten the ring? She was sooo lucky that no one noticed. At least if they did notice, they hadn't said anything yet. Yep, for the next few days she would just lay low.

Chapter 18

"Hey you, kid, stop!"

He was calling her. She just wanted to disappear and get back to Ruth and Faye. Boy, did she have a story to tell them. She hurried along the passage way but she could hear his steps catching up to her.

"Hey you, you're wearing my shirt. What's the big idea?"

He grabbed her by the suspenders and Rose came to a sudden halt. He removed her hat and suddenly all of her hair cascaded down.

"Rose, I knew it but I couldn't believe it? Why? What do you think you are doing?"

"I uh,"

"Never mind, I already know. I read your note you left for me. The whole family is beside themselves with worry. How could you do this? You know, you only think of yourself and not what the consequences of your actions might be on others."

"I did! I have! I sent them a postcard when we arrived in New York! And I did think about others. I thought how I didn't want to beat you in checkers back there because I wanted you to be the champion before your mates and also I wanted you to have something special before going to the war. I could-a beat you easy, and you know it!"

"Yeah, I know that. But that still doesn't excuse you from what you did to the family and especially to Mother. She is beside herself with worry, Rose. And, you stole my clothes! What's the meaning of that?"

"Dresses are not all that practical, you know, and I might find pants a lot more sensible in the desert."

"They're not going to let you wear pants over there, stupid girl. It's not like America, you know, where there are Annie Oakley's and other such wild women."

"I know, but still, I wanted a piece of you with me. Really I did!"

"Don't know if I believe that, baby sister!"

"Just because you were born a few minutes before me, doesn't make me your younger sister!"

"Well, I'd say that 20 minutes is nothing to sneeze at. I am definitely the older one and certainly a lot more mature."

"Oh pshaw! You are not!"

"Anyway, I'm not going to stand here and argue with you. You won't quit until you have won and this is not the time or place to get into that."

"Mark, I really am so glad to see you. I truly did not expect this and now I get to see you before you head to France. I want you to meet the Cohen's with whom I am traveling. You'll like Faye; she's our age. We are all so excited to get to Jerusalem so we can set up clinics and help the sick, poor and the wounded."

"It's so dangerous there, Rose. Why? You might even get ill yourself."

"Nah...I don't plan on that. I'm pretty tough you know. Remember you are the one who got chicken pox and the mumps and I didn't."

"Yes, well, still. It's not very safe there, either."

"I promise to be cautious and not take any chances. Really, I'm more worried about you. I don't know how you are going to fare in the trenches. There are diseases there, too. And, you have to keep your head down at all times or it might get...oh, I can't even say it. Just come back to us, ok? And, especially to Bertha; she must be nervous as a wild hen, poor thing."

"I'll be fine. I have vowed to come back in one piece so that Bertha and I can be married. She's already working on her wedding gown. Besides, the war is going to end soon. I might not even get into battle at all."

"Well, we are all hoping for that, I know. But anything could happen, so stay low, quiet, but foxy, brother."

"Yes, ma'am!"

"You know I'm not a mushy, gushy gal, but I just have to say that I don't know what I would do if something happened to you, Mark."

"I know, I feel the same about you, dear Rose. You are attached to my heart forever."

"Yeah, likewise."

Mark gave her a quick peck on the forehead and then turned away. It was the last she would see of him until they docked in England.

Chapter 19

As ship #19 made its way across the Atlantic, the passengers were becoming more aware of just how dangerous this voyage was. The world was at war and the Germans were keeping a fleet of U-boats in the Atlantic ready to sink any ship they took a fancy to. In peace time, this luxury liner was the S.S. Megantic. But now, great and grey, her only marking was a giant number "19" on her prow.

Three thousand American men and women occupied its berths and most were soldiers in khaki. Others were Red Cross and social welfare personnel. 44 passengers wore distinct badges with a red Star of David encircled by the words "American Zionist Medical Unit."

AZMU – as the Unit was popularly known – was long overdue. It was born two years previously, in June of 1916, when the World Zionist Organization in Copenhagen cabled an urgent appeal to send a medical force to Palestine.

Originally, the Unit was planned for two doctors, two nurses and a half-ton of supplies. However, by the time it got underway, there were over forty nurses and doctors, a pharmacist, and a sanitary engineer.

Henrietta Szold wanted to go but stayed behind to help raise funds. The supplies: vehicles, bedding, enough for a 50 bed hospital, were shipped separately. The two week crossing of the Atlantic was hard from the outset. Homesickness was aggravated by seasickness. Anxiety over submarines was so great that few of the members of the Unit undressed to sleep. Lifeboat drills were two and three times daily and only made their fears more real.

At 4 o'clock one morning close to Scotland's shore, sirens sounded the submarine alert. Members of the Unit hurried to their lifeboat stations.

Rose could only think of Mark and what he was doing at that very moment. They were huddled together in silence as the minutes passed by in agony. Ruth was holding on to Rose, and Faye was sandwiched in between her parents. They looked at one another as a thin glow of light on the horizon to the east began to lighten their faces. They all held the same thought: *We could have remained home. We are only volunteers. We don't have to be here. But this is a way to serve our country and our fellow Jews. We are on a mission of mercy.*

Rose thought that she could remain scared or move out of that reality and claim a different one. She decided that this would probably be the most exciting thing she had ever done and if she should survive, then the rest of the world would hear about it. She would report the adventure so others could really feel what it was like to be on a ship in the submarine infested waters of the Atlantic Ocean. She would look for a memento to take with her to remind herself of this very moment when she decided to go forth in confidence and not fear.

There were muffled explosions off in the distance and Rose said under her breath, "Go Get 'Em!" Ruth squeezed her hand tighter and Dr. Epstein motioned for her to keep silent. After what seemed an eternity, the "all-clear" horn sounded and they were free to go back to their cabins. The girls vowed to never take their clothes off again and would now sleep in their coats, boots, gloves and hats.

Dr. Cohen said, "Really girls, I think that is taking it a bit far!"

"No Sir," they shouted back. "Next time we will be ready for anything even if we hit an iceberg like the Titanic did."

"Now that is just not going to happen, so get some sleep. Breakfast time will be here sooner than you think."

It was while eating in the great dining room that the stories began to fly. Some were too odd to be true but most everyone agreed that their escort cruiser, the San Diego, spotted the sub and sank it. Everyone gave a cheer and Rose hurried through her eggs so she could get up on deck to check on Mark. Now that they were both on board, she just couldn't pretend that he did not exist. She did not care who found out. She would try to keep it a secret but her walking around in boy's clothing with the risk of being discovered could bring embarrassment not just to her but upon the Epstein's and the Cohen's. She really did not want to risk becoming enemies with them so early on in the trip.

Chapter 20

On June 24, 1918, #19 slipped into the Liverpool harbor. The girls marched down the gangplank holding both British and American flags that they had decided to make in honor of this momentous occasion. It had been two weeks since they had touched land and it felt that they still had the ocean beneath them even after they settled into the Regent Palace Hotel in London. For the next week they were escorted by London dignitaries to teas, parties, theaters and sightseeing excursions.

Rose saw Mark one more time before they docked and then she saw him from a distance as he disembarked with his troop and was led with the other soldiers to the military convoys waiting for them. It tugged at her heart that she would not know of his whereabouts for an unknown amount of time. He would not be able to write her, nor she, him. Her only way of knowing of his well-being was to write home with her new address in Jerusalem with hopes that they would forgive her enough to write her back. Of course, she was assuming that the postal service in Jerusalem was even predictable.

Oh well, she just couldn't spend time thinking about something that she had no control over. Mark had his job which was to push back the Turks and the Germans, and she had hers. And she was resolved to do the best that she could at whatever her responsibilities were to be. She and Mark had made a pact to be true to the *Dupen Family Honor* and make everyone proud with their good deeds and valor. Rose actually promised never to deceive her parents again and give them such a fright. Mark had helped her to see that her selfishness had caused more pain than she had realized.

She really admired Mark's courage and always respected his high sense of integrity. He was a good example of a perfect person that she realized she could never be. Actually, even though they were twins, there could never be two people that were so different. She loved and respected him, but really, his life was so predictable and somewhat boring. However, she would definitely try to be less immature in the pursuits of her future adventures.

But that is just what she wanted, lots of adventure in her life which only came by living on the edge and taking life on the fly. She couldn't and wouldn't plan every move as that would eliminate the unexpected which kept her sitting on the edge of her seat. The rush of the unknown was what kept this young lady from Chico, California, moving forward toward that big question mark, called life. She would stop at nothing less, for sure. *Just imagine the stories I will be able to tell!* She thought with a giggle.

One night, while attending a theater production that was primarily vaudevillian, Rose and the other girls sat arm-in-arm laughing so hard that they could hardly breathe. Then the most amazing thing happened. George Robey, the most incredible comedian, stopped the show, looked down at the audience and paid a wonderful tribute to the members of the AZMU volunteers. He asked them all to stand and give a wave. Then the audience stood and gave them a standing ovation. The girls huddled together giggling and turning red. Mrs. Cohen and Mrs. Epstein encouraged them to wave back to their admirers who were recognizing their efforts to help the stricken in Palestine.

But it was a long wait in London before they would be on the move again. Something was holding up the paperwork to leave the country. Rose overheard the adults discussing it all in hushed tones one night after hours. She snuck to the wall and listened intently and she heard that there was to be an important meeting the next night at the Royal London Opera House. *I want to be there to hear what all of this is about,* she thought.

The next day she let the others in on her plan. "Tonight there is going to be an important meeting at the Opera House about us going to Palestine. I think we should go."

"I think that our parents are planning to leave us here at the hotel," Ruth answered. "They will be going by themselves."

"Well, I want to go and see what is going on. We've been here two weeks and there has been no reason given for the delay. I'm tired of staying at the hotel here. Aren't you? Let's go and find out what is going on," Rose reasoned.

"We are lucky that the Opera House is not too far from here," Faye offered. "I'm curious too. It would be a nice adventure and it's perfect weather, plus there is a full moon to walk under. We'll wear our AZMU tags and we should be able to get in without any trouble."

"I guess, but I just don't know..." Ruth quavered.
"Ah, come on, Ruthie," Rose encouraged. "It'll be fun. Plus we'll find out what is really going on. I vote, yes!"

"Of course you would!" Ruth laughed. "Nothing could stop you from an adventure, that's for sure."

Faye offered the plan: "We will wait until after they leave. I think we should go out through the back so that the doorman does not see us, just in case he gets suspicious."

"Good idea, then we'll scoot on over to the theater and look very grown-up so as to pass by the ushers. I think we had better wear our hair up and under our hats. We need to look plain and serious. Don't look into anyone's eyes, either," Rose elaborated.

"My, have you done this before?" Faye asked. "Cuz you sound like a pro."

"She is, silly," Ruth snickered. "She just disguised herself so she could go up on deck and spy on the soldiers, remember?"

"Oh yeah, we are definitely with a pro, I see!" They worked on each other's hairdo's, wore the most mature dresses they could find, practiced their serious faces in the mirror, and then headed down the back stairs to the alley behind the hotel. They heard the cats running after the alley rodents and hurried out onto the roadway turning left onto the sidewalk and then walked until they neared the line of traffic that was backed up in hopes of finding parking lanes.

The London Bobbies (traffic police) were directing the horse-drawn buggies away from the automobiles and each were finding their own parking lots to settle in. Then more Bobbies were directing the pedestrians as they crossed Bow Street over to the theater.

It was a confusing sight but one that only excited the girls. The corners held vendors selling hot popcorn or hot sweet potatoes. There were still others with peanuts, chestnuts and cotton candy. It looked like the circus had come to town, but no, this was downtown London on a Saturday night, on a warm summer's eve.

Chapter 21

The first thing they noticed as they neared the Royal London Opera House was the great number of posters announcing the arrival of the AZMU. They read: "A Public Meeting to Welcome the American Zionist Medical Unit on its Way to Palestine". It was then that the three girls began to get an inkling of just how important they were. They were, indeed, a part of the American Zionist Medical Unit and they were planning on doing great things in Palestine.

They climbed the stairs up to the theater's entrance, calmly and directly walked through the doors with the rest of the visitors, walked across the lobby, followed a group heading to the left and then up a staircase to the fourth tier. Here they found some empty seats far above the stage that offered a view of almost every row in the three tiers below them and then on to the ground floor or loge. They saw the boxes to the right and left of the stage filled with dignitaries, of whom they knew not, but surmised as much since they were standing and waving to those in the loges.

It was inspiring to be in such a grand place that was so old and whose walls had heard such famous dignitaries like kings and queens, let alone the dramatic voices of the Puccini and Verdi operas. Their seats had held countless Londoners for a century before their arrival, and the awareness of this was awe inspiring to these girls from Chico, California. They held each other's hands as a kind of protection against, or one might say, proof that this very moment was indeed happening to them.

Rose felt a tingle go up her spine. She knew that feeling. It happened whenever she went out too far on the branch of the tree in the back yard. It happened when she took a dare and knew that it was questionable if she could do it. It happened when she lifted herself out of her regular old self and forced a new and daring moment upon herself. It was happening now.

The evening moved through several speakers who were praising the new homeland in Palestine being set aside for the Jews. These were the Zionists who had already been there to meet with the Arab people in order to make way for the influx of Jews to follow. The Rothschild Hospital was well established in Jerusalem and in two weeks' time the cornerstone for the Hebrew University would be laid. They cheered on the AZMU group and stated that the work they would do in this long-oppressed and down-trodden area was a great tribute to the modern Zionists who were seeking ways to solve the problems of New Palestine.

The girls looked at one another and were proud that they had worn their AZMU badges. This would show the Londoners that they were part of a group of people who could be considered heroes and heroines.

After about an hour, Rose felt that it was time to sneak back into their hotel before the adults returned. They quickly rose from their seats and tiptoed back down the stairs to the main floor. The lobby was still and quiet, and the voice booming from the stage could be heard. *And I say to you,* they heard. *That the Balfour Declaration is the "Magna Charta" of the Jewish people, and it is these people of the Jewish Medical Unit that are the beginning of it.*

Yes, Rose's dream had come true. She was living on the cutting edge right here and right now. She hoped that she would remember everything about this moment, the smells, the colors, the sounds and the excitement that was traveling up and down her spine.

Chapter 22

The truth was that the journey to Palestine was going very slowly. There were numerous hold-ups concerning paper work, available room on trains and ships, and then the submarine raid in the Mediterranean which delayed them for 10 days. On August 11, they arrived in Alexandria, Egypt aboard an Indian transport, the *Kaiser I. Hind* but not without another fright.

Rose thought that she had seen enough water for one life time and was anxiously waiting for the first vision of Alexandria where they would be docking. It was hot out on deck just as they had been warned it would be when they arrived in North Africa. She thought back over the last two months of travel and the old phrase *like a slow boat to China*...entered her mind. This trip had been like a slow boat to China with all of the stops and waits that went on. But soon that would be over with and upon Egyptian soil she would place her finely booted foot.

Faye and Ruth burst out from the dining room to join Rose gazing out onto the emptiness of the sea filled with the anticipation of seeing the first sign of land. They came beside her and snuggled in keeping Rose in the middle.

"Are you thinking about Mark, Rose?" asked Ruth. "Wondering where he is?"

"I could be, but I'm not," she answered. "I'm thinking about being on a slow boat to China and how this journey to Palestine still is not over yet and we have been traveling for two months. I really thought that we would be back home in Chico by now. It's a great adventure, but I just want to be in Palestine now so we can get to work.

Plus, I'm just dying to use my Hebrew and practice my bandaging skills. I do wonder about Mark from time to time, but not too much since there is nothing I can do about his situation and why waste energy thinking unproductive thoughts when there is nothing I can do. I just hope that he is ok, of course."

"Father said that we should be seeing land within the next hour or two," Faye said. "So we decided to come out here with you and find it together. It's kind of like a treasure hunt...you know, who will see the first speck of land first."

"I feel like Noah," Ruth added. "We should look for the dove with a twig in its beak showing us that land is near. That's what I'm going to look for."

"Hmm, I was thinking that I should go back to the cabin to pack up my things," Rose commented. "I want to be rea..."

And she did not get a chance to finish her sentence because the sirens blew and there was a scurrying about. They were ordered to go to their cabins and put on their life belts and then they would be told what to do next. The girls looked at each other and the same thought passed through their heads at the same time. No, they were not going to their cabins during this one last raid. They aimed to get themselves somewhere so they could actually see what was going to take place.

Rose led the way to a spot she had discovered while poking around the outside decks. It was a trap door in the floor that led to a tiny room with a tiny porthole. It appeared to be storing kegs of nails and other construction items probably used for emergency repairs.

They entered the darkness and squeezed in around the tiny window to have a view of the waters. These sirens meant that more submarines had been sighted and that all must be prepared for a possible attack. Rose had never grown bored with the many submarine raids that had taken place on their ship journeys. They, actually, were the highlight of the voyages for her. *I must be absolutely daft to think that! But who cares. Life is to be lived with gusto and I aim to do just that,* she giggled to herself.

"Look, look!" Ruth said tapping the glass of the porthole. "I think I see a submarine!"

"I think they are taking quite a chance coming in so close to Alexandria," Faye said with disdain in her voice. "They don't know that they will be shot in two seconds if they keep this up."

"You tell them, Faye," Rose giggled.

They could hear the crew running to their battle stations. It's true that the parents would be worried because the girls would not show up at their cabins, but this last raid before docking was too good to pass up. They stayed glued to the porthole watching for any little sign of a sub and it wasn't long before they saw what they thought was a thin pipe coming up out of the water. Yes, it was a sub with its periscope up and looking around.

"Ok, shoot 'em," Ruth yelled out to the crew.

"Ruth, it's not a Wild West show, you know. Our guys won't fire until they are absolutely sure that we will be attacked. We don't have enough firepower aboard to make much of a dent in a submarine fleet, you know," Rose cautioned.

At that moment, there was a sound of a cannon shot leaving the deck and the girls looked at each other, then back out onto the sea just in time to see an explosion just ahead of them.

"I bet that was a warning shot that we gave them, Miss Smarty!" Ruth giggled.

"Hmm, could be, but, I don't know why we would do that," Rose answered.

"I think that it is a signal to other boats in the area to come toward us to be an escort for us." Faye said thoughtfully. "Remember, that's what the *USS Nevada* did for us as we were nearing Scotland."

"Yeah, that's what I mean," Ruth continued. "It's a show of power – Like President Roosevelt said, *walk softly but carry a big stick.*"

"I don't call shooting off a cannon walking softly," Rose muttered.

Within the hour, the all-clear siren blew and the girls hurried along the passage ways to their cabins. It was true that several other ships appeared on the horizon as a total of 5 cannon shots rang off the bow of the ship. They boldly escorted the *Kaiser I. Hind* into the Alexandria harbor. But the real fireworks began when the girls returned to their parents. They knew that they would find two sets of very worried parents and this time there were consequences for their cheekiness in ignoring the orders of the Captain. Their bedtimes would now be moved up to 6 p.m. and the rest of the time they would need one or more of the parents as an escort.

For the first few days in Alexandria this was effective, but soon, the girls would need to move away from the parents and work independently of them and perform as the medical personnel they were supposed to be. The girls were apologetic enough but often said later that the last submarine raid of all was the very best! And that is exactly what they each wrote in their diaries.

Chapter 23

Egypt in the summer is hot and dry. The girls knew about hot summers in the Sacramento Valley, but summers in the desert, even if there was an oasis, was a different kind of heat. It was drier and void of the valley trees the girls were used to seeing. They liked the palm trees with their sweet coconuts, but the best was the pomegranates. The few days they spent in Cairo was filled with explorations of the hotel grounds, the open-air market place, and the various food venders along the street.

Rose was shocked by the large numbers of young children wandering around hoping and asking for money, but mostly trying to sell them a trinket or two. They seemed to know just enough English to get what they wanted; they were desperate for even the smallest coins.

The conditions of the poor never left Rose's memory for the rest of her life. There were mud huts along the Nile, sickly peasants working the earth, rotting refuse in the streets, blind beggars, and everywhere there were swarms of flies spreading an invisible germ canopy over the entire city.

The desert conditions brought sand everywhere including the inside of their hotel room and eventually on every piece of clothing. Of course the slightest breeze brought the tiny particles right through the window sashes. There did not appear to be any defense against the sand ending up inside their bed covers.

Rose's diary entry read:

Arrived in Cairo, Egypt, and soon was covered in sand from head to toe. The worse is when the wind blows and the sand is swept up and cascades through the air and lands in my mouth, eyes, and ears. Even the food has a special crunch to it as the tiny silica finds its way into my bowl. I sure hope sand in the tummy doesn't play havoc and present me with a royal stomach ache!

I refuse to say that I am homesick for Chico, but I am feeling unprepared for this latest adventure. I watch the natives manage their lives in this sandy home and I think that I just have to persevere and figure out how to greet the sandy life as a friend rather than a foe. But I have to say that the poverty and the poor children who are suffering from it make me want to cry. Besides the sand everywhere there are flies and more flies that invade every space that exists. We have to cover our heads and faces just to be free of them. Our beds are covered in a tent of netting.

So far, the hotel workers here at the Shepeard Hotel have been quite helpful in getting us our food and good water. They also seem happy and fun loving. Some even speak to us in English which is a relief since sign language is not my best talent.

But both Ruth and Faye agree with me that the hardest thing to take in so far, are the children who are dirty and poor. They appear to be very hungry and not too healthy. The girls and I save little items from our meal plates for them, but it never seems to be enough.

Yesterday we walked along the edge of the Nile which was a great experience because I have read about this mighty river in our school books but to actually see it, touch it and smell it was far beyond any words that could describe it. We stopped for a while and looked out on this passage way of water that once held boats belonging to the Pharaohs and Queens like Cleopatra. Faye said that we should imagine this mighty river turned to blood as it had when Moses was trying to free the Jews from Egypt. The Nile turning to blood was one of the mighty seven plagues that Moses used to punish Pharaoh. That really would have been amazing to see. For a moment I wished that I could go back in time and be an eyewitness.

At times I am impatient with the many delays we have endured on this trip, but I guess that it is out of our control since we are traveling in war time and smooth passage from one place to another is rather difficult to come by. We have seen some camels, though, and we or I am intent on finding out how we can ride one. I think the Cohens and the Epsteins want to do that also, so at least I don't have to sneak out on my own. Really, I have not come all this way to NOT ride a camel!

We have seen a lot of soldiers walking the streets and they seem curious about us and our western dress. We've heard that they are here in the city because they are guarding the food and water supplies for the soldiers in the field. All I know is that some of them are real cute and that they like to try to get our attention. Earlier today, three of them brought us ice cream cones and wanted to walk us along the path by the river. The mothers immediately said 'no' and rushed us back to the hotel. This irritated me as I was looking forward to getting to know them. They were very nice, I thought, but I was outnumbered and had to follow the girls. Well, this time I gave in, but next time I think I will plan to talk to these men; if there is a next time. I've realized that soldiers are moved around so much that you hardly get to see the same one twice.

As usual, here is my list of the ten unique things that I have noticed about Egyptian life and, as usual, I will not list the language as that is a given everywhere I go!

1) So different from England, France and Italy as we are in a REAL desert now!

2) We hear the call to prayer from the mosques every day. This is the first time I have been in a country that is not Christian.

3) The clothing is not traditional. Even though I had expected to see everyone in long robes, called Brukhas, it was not until the first day when I saw streets of people in them that the difference really hit me.

4) I think that every single man I have seen that is Egyptian has a beard.

5) The women always cover most of their faces when they are on the street.

6) These Egyptians are very, very polite.

7) There are many, many animals on the streets as well as people.

8) The food is so different but I love it. There are different grains and fruits. My new best friend is the pomegranate!

9) *The open air market is very fun and colorful.*

And last, but definitely not least, Dear Diary, I want to ride a camel!!!!
We have been promised a ride tomorrow, but I have learned to not believe promises too much anymore since we have been on this trip. The fact that the sun sets every evening and rises every morning is all the promises we get these days. I understand how uncertain life during war time can be, but it is even more uncertain now that we are in the Middle East.
I'm signing off now and I hope to slip into slumber land now. I am still thinking about the poor children on the street and am hoping that they find a nice place in which to sleep.

Rose Caty Dupen

Chapter 24

Once again they were awakened by the call to prayer from the mosque.

The heat had enveloped the girls and had given them a fitful sleep until a breeze off of the Nile finally filled their hotel room at about 2 a.m. Rose had decided to slip out of bed after several attempts to fall asleep. First of all, it was just too hard to settle down after their afternoon camel ride. Dr. Epstein had finally found a camel owner who would be willing to take them all for a ride around the hotel courtyard. It was a large area filled with palm trees and grass that seemed like an oasis in the desert as it offered relief to the eye from the bright, white buildings surrounding it.

The owner was an Englishman who had come to Egypt thirty years earlier and had gotten into the transport business running a string of pack camels across the desert. Dr. Epstein had met him at the market place and it was such a pleasure to speak with someone who knew English that they had visited for over an hour while sipping hot, rich, Turkish coffee.

At 3 p.m. Johnson, as the camel owner was called, showed up at the courtyard. He insisted that the girls cover their heads as was the custom for the Arab women.

Ruth was the first up onto the critter's back. He was down on the ground waiting while Johnson put a stool next to him. She climbed onto the stool and her father gave her a boost up onto its back. Rose sat in the middle and Faye was at the back. Ruth held onto the wooden handle protruding from the seat but the reins extended down to Johnson who was to lead Malcolm around the pathway. Yes, Malcolm was named for Johnson's best mate when they were in the Royal Navy together.

"Is he going to spit, Johnson?" Faye asked. "I read that they spit at you if they are mad. Is that true?"

"Not to worry young lady," he answered. "If Malcolm decides to show his mean side it will be at me, not you three flowers of the desert."

Johnson gave the command to rise and as Malcolm straightened his back legs to a standing position, the three girls were thrust forward toward his neck. They squealed and grabbed hold of each other in hopes that they would not topple down over his head onto the ground. Ruth bent over and hugged his neck, and before they knew it Malcolm thrust out his front legs and the girls rose into the air and leveled out on Malcolm's back. Johnson gave him encouraging words and patted his long neck. Malcolm said that he was not too happy about getting up from his resting position with these three noisy girls on his back but Johnson merely told him that he was being silly and that he was to act nice. This huge ship of the desert shook his head and a froth of foam slipped out of his muzzle and sprayed his unsuspecting passengers. Unfortunately, Ruth, being in the front, got the bulk of the spray and yelled the loudest, "Oh no! I'm covered in green slime!"

Rose added to the cacophony by yelling that he was spitting at them because he was mad and Faye just tucked her head into Rose's back to avoid the green slop.

"Ah girls, that's just normal," Johnson reassured them. "Remember that these animals have several stomachs and spend a lot of time rc-chewing their food. It won't hurt you, I assure you! Besides, you look most becoming with your new green paint, ha, ha! Ok, Malcolm, let's show these girls a good turn around this lovely garden here."

Malcolm moved forward rocking and rolling around the pathway. The girls were soon moving to and fro like they would on a horse, but there was also a rolling motion that resembled the feeling of being on a ship.

Rose started with a giggle, "Hey, I thought we were off the boat. I feel like I'm back on it now."

"I knew that we would be up off the ground, but this is farther up than I thought," stated Faye.

"Well, I think old Malcolm here smells like wet grass." Ruth added.

"You probably only smell all that green stuff on your dress, Ruth," Rose laughed.

"Oh my," Ruth laughed back, "you are probably right!"

Dr. Epstein walked beside Johnson chatting about the transport business and how much it had picked up because of the war. There was always some group wanting things delivered either to the east or west. Sometimes he went up the Nile, but mostly those deliveries were handled by the river boats.

It seemed as if everything was going along without a hitch when Malcolm threw his head, let out a bellow and would not move forward. They were stopped and he had no intention of moving. Johnson called and whistled, yelled and cooed to Malcolm but nothing worked. Even Dr. Epstein helped to pull on the rope but Malcolm would not budge.

"I was afraid of this," Johnson shook his head and yelled into Malcolm's ear, "I going to sell you to the meat factory. Get going, now!"

The large furry desert ship had no intention of moving. It was as if his four feet were cemented to the ground. Rose had an idea and started talking to this stubborn creature in a little cooing voice, "It's alright, Malcolm. Just take us around one more time and then you can go back to the stable with your friend Johnson, here."

"Ruth," she said. "Scoot on up his neck and start tickling his ears. He will think that there are flies attacking him and he will want to walk away from them. I've done this at home when our horse gets stubborn, and it really works."

So Ruth moved up onto Malcolm's neck stretched out to reach his ears and then began tickling the little hairs protruding outward. At first Malcolm did nothing but then his ears began to move forward and backwards as if he was bothered by something. He shook his head and then moved it up and down in a fast manner, as if he was trying to rid himself of something.

"See," Rose whispered. "It's working. Soon he will want to move from this spot and get away from the big fly called Ruth!"

It wasn't long before the girls felt the big desert ship move forward. He didn't stop again as it appeared that as long as he was moving then he would not be bothered by the big 'Ruth Fly'!

Ten minutes later Johnson brought old Malcolm to a halt and ordered him down on his knees. They disembarked in the opposite order with Faye getting off first. They complimented Malcolm for such a lovely ride and Rose leaned over and gave him a peck on the muzzle. She pulled out of her pocket a sugar cube and slipped it in his mouth.

"Malcolm just needs to know that he's special and that we like him," said Rose. "I like you Malcolm, you are a good camel."

"Well, girls, say goodbye to Johnson and we'll just get back in time to change your 'green' dresses for dinner," Dr. Epstein ordered. "Johnson, it's been a pleasure spending this time with you. You are an interesting fella with many stories to tell."

"Well, sir," Johnson answered. "The pleasure's been mine, especially since I learned something about Malcolm here today...the next time he freezes in the pathway, I'll just whisper sweet words in his ears and then tickle them. Thank you, Miss, for that excellent bit of information! Good luck in Jerusalem and be careful over there. There are some wild bandits who think that whatever they want is theirs for the taking."

Chapter 25

By Saturday evening, August 17, 1918, the British had
cleared space on a troop train in order to send AZMU on the
last leg if its voyage to Palestine. The group boarded a double-
decker berthed train and traveled the route into the Holy Land
chosen by Moses to free the Israelites from Pharaoh. Across
the horizon as they chugged along in the bright moonlight,
they could make out long caravans of camels.

By the early morning they had crossed the Suez Canal
and were in Kantara. The northern coast of Sinai, along the
Mediterranean was anything but pleasant; a sandstorm
swirled up out of the desert and all views were lost in the
gritty winds.

Eighteen hours after they started out, the train finally
arrived in Lydda, a sandy tent town that did not have one
shade tree. They debarked to wait for someone to pick them
up, but it appeared that they had been forgotten for it was two
hours later that they were finally summoned.
Ruth, Rose and Faye were trying to stay positive in the desert
heat, but even though they were used to the hot summers in
the Sacramento Valley, Lydda offered an oppressive heat
coupled with a wind that was full of sand.

They were taken to Tel Aviv, not Jerusalem as the
agreement was for AZMU to establish their base there and
then to send a detachment on to Jerusalem. The vehicles
ferried them through the desert on limestone roads and past
the citrus groves to Tel Aviv. They arrived at the three houses
that they would occupy located at the edge of town. Beyond
the houses were only sand dunes.

The seven from California gathered their valises and entered the house where they were assigned. Besides mounds of sand exhibiting itself in most every corner of the little dwelling, the place was large enough to accommodate them comfortably with a bedroom left over for two other nurses to occupy. Annie from Boston and Julie from New York City were happy to share a room. Anything was better than the berth they had on that long train ride.

Of course, the flies were everywhere and soon the netting was placed over the beds and hung at the doors and windows. The rest of the supplies were brought in and the girls were put to work scrubbing from top to bottom. It was 95 degrees outside so it was not long before the girls were dumping the buckets of water over each other in an attempt to cool off. By supper they had sufficiently cleaned their little abode; made the beds; sanitized the kitchen area; and started a large pot of vegetable soup. They would not partake in any meat tonight, but they all hoped that tomorrow would bring a successful meeting with a butcher in town.

Everyone was exhausted from the long train ride; the two hour wait at the station in Lydda; and the hours spent making their little hovel livable; so without much conversation these girls were lying atop their beds fast asleep.

All, that is, for Rose Dupen who had a date with her diary. She just could not let another minute pass without jotting down her first impressions of the Holy Land.

Dear Diary,

I just couldn't write on that awful train as it jiggled and jumped along from Cairo, to Lydda in Palestine. Why, we could hardly walk up and down the aisle without falling over onto someone.

We tried to sleep in our berths but they rocked and jumped us into total frustration. I finally slept after Faye suggested that we try to imagine what the motion of the train could be, if we did not know that we were on a train. That was fun and kept our minds off of our misery. I thought the whole motion would resemble what it would feel like if someone threw me up and down with a blanket like the Eskimos do in the far north. That idea made everyone laugh.

We arrived in Lydda and were unloaded with all of our valises, supplies and equipment in front of the railway station which was a little shack. The wind was blowing and so was the sand. The heat was unbearable and we almost collapsed because of it. In fact two nurses actually fainted from lack of sleep and the oppressive heat.

After two hours of waiting, we were picked up and taken to Tel Aviv. There had been a change in plans and we were to station ourselves there instead of Jerusalem. It had something to do with politics and the Zionists but I did not truly understand it. All I know is that we have our work cut out for us since the living conditions are worse than poverty, if that is possible.

Our house is one of three given to the AZMU's located at the edge of town. We are deep in the desert here and I can't imagine that this town will amount to much. Personally, I wouldn't send anyone to live here.

But I've been negative, that's true. I guess that I just have to get it out of my system before I can tell you about some of the unique things here. After cleaning our abode from top to bottom; hanging the netting over the beds and doors; and making a nice pot of soup; we gathered around the table and it became so quiet that we could hear the sand stirring on the window sills. We were thinking of our homes back in America and realizing where we are now, at least, that is what I was doing. I reminded myself that I wanted to be on the cutting edge of life and that is exactly where I am. Boy, what squalor and filth. I didn't know that the cutting edge would be so inhospitable.

I am thinking about the 10 different things I have noticed about the life in the Holy Land, but, since I just arrived, I don't have many yet. But one thing for sure is that they may call this the Holy Land, but it does not feel holy to me. It is dirty, sandy, hot, and very poor. I do not know how the common person can survive such difficult conditions.

I feel sleep finally overtaking me, and I am thankful that my bed is not rocking and rolling like it was on the train. Tomorrow should dawn in a better light and I hope to have a more positive report for you then.

Rose Caty Dupen

Chapter 26

Within days the girls were busy setting up a sanitary unit in Jaffa. Tel Aviv and Jaffa were close neighbors so it was not far to travel between them. They supervised garbage collection; over saw food inspections; and also set up supervisors for malaria control. Rose immediately sent a letter back home now that she had a permanent address. She had sent letters from London, Paris, and Cairo, but now at least, she hoped that she would receive something in return since now she could actually send them an address.

My Dearest Mother and Father,

It is August 25th in Tel Aviv, Palestine. We arrived via an overnight train from Cairo to Lydda and then by transport trucks to Tel Aviv. Everywhere we look we see the effects of war, famine, and disease. We pity these poor ones who have endured so much.

We are safe, well-fed, and set up in our own little house on the edge of town. So far we have been deployed to Jaffa, a settlement nearby, to help with the set-up of a sanitary unit. When we drove down the sandy streets, many came out of their homes to welcome us with a cheer. For a minute we felt very special, but soon we had to get to the business at hand and try to bring a better life to these poor residents.

I am wondering if you have heard from Mark. I know that you probably received my other letters; at least I hope that you have. But you were not able to send me anything since I had no address. Now that I am settled for a while, you will be able to send all letters here.

So now I would like to know how everyone is. I already know that I gave you quite a scare by sneaking off with the Epstein's to the Middle East, so you don't have to tell me about that. I am sorry for scaring you but really, this adventure is proving to be an incredible experience and I feel that I am actually helping people who really need saving. I am glad that I am here. I just hope that you will find it in your hearts to forgive me for disobeying you.

Meanwhile, soon will be our supper and I am in charge of the meal tonight: lentil stew with couscous. You can imagine all of the different foods I have tried on this trip. Some have been pleasing while others are not worth mentioning. Couscous is a grain that cooks quickly and is filling and has a mild taste. There are also groves of olive trees here and other groves of citrus. Pomegranates are most popular as are the coconuts. But I really am in love with the figs and pomegranates.

I hope that this letter finds you well and enjoying the end of summer. Tell everyone that I am well, missing them but am very happy to be here helping as much as I can. I worry about my brothers but trust that you will inform me of their safety and whereabouts.

With best wishes to everyone and love to you, Mother and Father,

Your youngest daughter, Rose

There, that should do it, she thought. She would post it tomorrow on the way to Jaffa. They would be visiting the clinic in there to take a head count and to replenish their supplies. Yesterday more medical supplies arrived from New York so now they could start equipping all of the clinics.

Chapter 27

"I have come to the conclusion," Eli Epstein said as they were beginning their late dinner. "That if we did not have our interpreters here alongside of us that we would be rendered helpless. Don't the rest of you agree?"

"Well, we are just getting our feet wet," Daniel Cohen added. "But yes, it has been a great help. I know some Hebrew, no Arabic or French, but somehow, a stomach ache is a stomach ache in any language! Am I right?"

"I wish there was something that we could do about the fleas and flies," Rachel Epstein added. "They aggravate me and everyone else to death!"

"I don't know how these poor women cope," Anne Cohen shook her head. "There is no clean place in which to give birth."

"Girls, these conditions should open your eyes to the filth and pestilence that some people have to endure," Dr. Epstein looked at Ruth, Rose and Faye sitting across from the four parents.

It was 10 p.m. and a hot meal was finally hitting their stomachs. Their little hovel had an adequate kitchen area that held a rickety board table with two long benches on either side of it. The girls always sat on one side while the parents faced them on the other. The place was primitive but they were making do. With no hot water they kept a kettle on the gas burner for washing dishes, baths, and rinsing out their shirts and skirts from one day to the next.

Rose was once again thankful that she had brought Mark's pants and shirt since trying to rinse out a long skirt was next to impossible. Besides, she had noticed that Faye and Ruth would invariably walk with a dust cloud behind them because their skirts would swish from side to side and kick up the sand. The natives were not pleased with a girl wearing pants but Rose just stuck her stubborn chin out and proceeded with the medical procedure that they needed. By the end of the day it did not matter what she was wearing as the patients were so thankful to have found help and relief.

Whereas they all wanted to be in Jerusalem with the other half of the team, they found that Tel Aviv and Jaffa were so needy that they could not think of leaving. They had made friends with the Arabs and Jews alike and were generously paid with fresh fruits, vegetables, goat milk and cheese, plus dozens of eggs. They could not complain about an inadequate amount of food, they just complained that they could not keep it fresh or the clinic sanitary. They had decided that eating fresh meat would be questionable since there was no refrigeration. They would, however, consider jerky since it was dried.

Mostly their diet consisted of the fruits and vegetables with cooked grains and a slice or two of cheese. No one complained but privately they were wishing that they had gone for that steak on the menu in Paris when they were there several weeks ago.

Water was a problem in that it needed to be boiled before drinking. They were warned that drinking the water could possibly introduce bacteria that could bring on a severe case of diarrhea.

"I heard today that so many homes were destroyed in the last battle here that the families have had to double and triple up in the existing houses that are still standing," Rose commented.

"Yes, the children look so sad," Ruth added. "It just wants to make me cry along with them."

"Have more meds arrived for their trachoma, Father?" Faye asked.

"It should be here tomorrow which is what I have been hearing for the last week," Daniel answered.

"I see the disease," Ruth said. "But I don't understand what it is or how they get it. What is it Dr. Cohen?"

"That's a good question, Ruth," Daniel answered. "I'm sure that you have heard of 'Pink Eye?' You were told in school not to touch anyone's books if they had the disease. It is very contagious and the eyes become pink and itchy to the point of being sore. Well, left untreated it can cause further problems and eventually lead to blindness."

"Why do so many have it here?" Faye asked.

"The living conditions have become unsanitary, crowded and infested with flies and these are the ways that the disease is spread," continued Eli. "Without immediate treatment and a change in cleanliness, the disease will continue to plague these poor people. They have not had access to proper medication and so they have not been able to wipe out the disease. Now that we are here, perhaps we can bring some positive changes."

"But there are so many of them, Daniel," commented Anne. "How are we ever going to get to them all?"

"I agree," Rachel concurred, "We can't possibly get to them all."

Eli shook his head, "That is the whole problem. There just are not enough of us or of medical supplies. We can only do as much as we can every day. That is why we must make each day count."

Rose got up from the table and walked outside. She felt the warm breeze caressing her skin and immediately she felt a chill travel up her back to the top of her head. *Uh oh*, she knew what that meant. Whenever that happened she knew that some big change was about to happen. It was like a psychic wind that blew through her bones to let her know that she was going to be called on for an important task. She couldn't imagine what it would be as she was already in the middle of an important task. But something was going to happen and it would not be long before she would find out.

It was a crescent moon that night and she imagined the family in Chico looking at the same moon, and then she realized that Mark was seeing the same moon as he sat in the trenches somewhere in France. Sam and Adam, wherever they were on the battlefront, were under this same sliver orb wondering if the end would ever come to this awful war.

Yes, it's coming dear brothers. Soon we will all be back home sitting around our big table sharing one of our wonderful Dupen meals. There were so many Dupens now that Father and Mother had purchased another table to set up in the parlor when all of them gathered.

She wasn't homesick but she was in such a different place than Chico, California, that it was hard to comprehend that they were still on the same planet.

Chapter 28

Tomorrow, Dear Diary, we are moving to Jerusalem. They need more Aides there at the Rothschild Hospital and the adults think that we can be spared from Jaffa. Actually, this is exactly what I wanted. I did not picture myself in a filthy town like Tel Aviv or Jaffa. I wanted to be in the heart of the country: Jerusalem. That is the city where so much history has taken place and is still happening. I want to walk along the streets where Bible heroes walked and lived. I want to touch what is left of the great temple wall and to see the old Jerusalem next to the modern one. This is where the real cutting edge is. This is where I will find my story.

t's been a week since I last wrote and besides the day to day routines of cooking and cleaning and fighting off the flies, we have been treating hundreds of children with that awful Trachoma eye disease. We have to be very careful ourselves to keep clean and free from contact, but that is next to impossible. The heat has been unbearable with the mosquitos swarming and spreading that dreaded disease, malaria. I know all about malaria as we unfortunately have to deal with it in Chico.

My Hebrew is improving as is my Arabic, but only a few very necessary words to get me by are sticking with me. Mostly I am teaching the patients English; they want to know more now that the British are arriving after the defeat of the Turks.

We will be staying right where the hospital is as there are some dorms there for the resident doctors. I am excited about going as we will be on our own except for some other nurses going with us. This is the first time that we will be left to our own judgments and I feel that I am ready.

So, lights out, Dear Diary as we leave at 5 a.m. before the heat overwhelms us.

Rose Caty Dupen

The girls were up at the first call and washed their faces, combed their hair into a bun, affixed their sun hats and hurried down hot tea with a piece of flat bread topped with a hunk of cheese. The sky was lightening ever so slightly as they found their spots in the open-air small bus that was to ferry them to Jerusalem. They would probably arrive by the middle of the afternoon. They had brought along something to read for the journey but the road was so rutted that the jumping and jostling of the vehicle kept their eyes from focusing on anything.

Ruth and Faye had found a family with 2 children and were having fun with them playing finger games. Rose starred out on the bleakness of the desert and tried to picture it with groves of citrus and nut trees. She had heard the other adults talking about the dream of turning the desert into a 'Garden of Eden' once they were able to pump water to it. It was hard to believe that anything at all could grow there. She supposed that it would be a miracle if abundance actually came from this desolate place.

She spied caravans of camels loaded with bulging packs lumbering towards them no doubt heading for the large markets of Jerusalem. There were men atop them as well as those running alongside. Now, that was something only the Bedouins of the desert had stamina for. She tried to look closely to see if this was just a trip for business or if whole families were included. It was too hard to tell, but she thought that she caught sight of some very small figures that could have been the children. Even they were heartily traipsing through the hot sands. *I certainly hope that we stop for water soon.* She thought to herself. *Of course, where is the water, is the next obvious question.*

Within the hour they spotted a cluster of trees in the distance. Finally, they would get to experience a 'real' oasis like they had read about in their history books. It was a place like no other they had seen on their travels. Suddenly they were transported into another world of greenery, lushness, and water. There was a well and running water into a pool. Many tracks could be seen where others had gathered around to quench their thirst.

Faye was the first one. She took a hand full of water and put it up to her mouth for a cool drink. Her second motion was a little different, though. She took that hand full of water and threw it in the direction of Rose. Of course, it landed on her nose which caused her to scream in surprise, gather up her own hand full and then splash it back at Faye, missed but ended up splashing Ruth in the ear. By that time the three girls were squealing and laughing as water was flying everywhere. When they finally couldn't stop laughing and could therefore not splash any more water, they fell on to the ground and held their sides in laughing pain.

"Oh my," Ruth exclaimed, "that felt so good! I haven't laughed so much in a long time. I think we needed that!"

"We've been so busy caring for the desperate ones that I've forgotten that there is a whole other side of life to experience!" Rose added.

"I thought we needed a good shaking up," Faye confessed. "After all those hours traveling through the desert I could see the color leaving our faces. Come on, let's wash up and face the rest of the day with vigor!"

They then went arm-in-arm back to the bus singing: Yankee Doodle...!

Chapter 29

They were dropped off at the Rothschild Hospital and were shown their dorm where they would share their quarters with 10 other women from AZMU. There was not a lot of privacy but they were young and could handle a little bit of openness among girls.

The Great Ward, as the room was called, held 14 beds, 7 along opposite walls. On each end were doors that either led to another hallway or to the communal bath. It was clean enough and somehow the fly problem was next to non-existent.

The three girls were lucky to find beds along the south wall next to each other. Each bed had drawers underneath for some of their things as well as a cupboard over the headboard. There was just enough room to fit everything they had brought. They arrived at 2 p.m. so there was still plenty of time to go exploring. The Great Hall was located on the west side of the hospital and the hallway in which they had arrived was begging for exploration.

"Let's go down this way and see what we can find," Rose suggested.

They passed rooms housing offices and one great room that appeared to be a library. The doors were closed but they could peek through the little window and see what appeared to be doctors reading books perhaps researching the latest treatment for a particular case they were treating. They didn't want to disturb them so they moved on down the hall. The floor was painted a light green and the walls were bright white so that if there was a fingerprint left by an unsuspecting hand, it could be found and easily removed. The girls were impressed with the cleanliness everywhere.

"I wonder where we will be stationed," Ruth queried. "I overheard the others say that there would be a meeting tonight to inform us of our duties," Faye stated.

"Oh look," Rose said, "another hallway. Let's go that way. Now someone keep track of how many turns we are making and which way we are going! We don't need to be lost the very first day we get here!"

This hallway had a nice feature to it in that the floors had been painted a light brown so all the girls needed to remember was that they went from the green hallway to the brown one. The rooms they passed were closed and dark on the other side so they did not venture up on their toes to see into the little window at the top of the door. At the end of the hall there was an abrupt right that led them down another one only with a yellow painted floor...so green, brown, yellow...they all said to themselves.

That hallway was darker and had 4 doors. But at the end were large double doors painted blue. The blue doors looked very important. They had small windows at the top. There was a light on so the girls would be able to see what was inside. As they rose on their toes and leaned into the window, one of the doors was pushed ajar.

They looked at each other with surprise and Rose was the first to say what they were all thinking. "I'm going in. I have my AZMU badge on so I can announce who I am and simply say that I got a little turned around. Are you girls coming with me?"

"Gee, golly, I mean," Ruth stuttered. "Is this another one of your adventures, Rose?"

"I think it's a great idea," Faye piped up. "I'll go with you, Rose."

"Well, you're not going to leave me here alone, so I guess I'm coming," Ruth said begrudgingly.

Rose opened the door wider and slipped into the room quietly with the other two following her. There was an office off to the right, but no one was in there. There was a desk piled with papers and something that looked like an ancient typewriter. They walked passed and into a larger room with six or seven gurneys, or portable beds. They looked normal but what was on top of them was not. There were large lumps covered with white sheets. Much to their surprise, they resembled the size of a person.

"Oh," Ruth gasped, "where are we?"

"I know," Rose whispered, "but I don't want to say. It's kind of creepy."

"It's the morgue; we've walked into the morgue!" Faye exclaimed in a voice just above a whisper.

"Oh my goodness, Oh my goodness, Oh my goodness," Ruth loudly whispered in shock.

"I'm going to look at one," Rose boldly said, "I've never seen a corpse and there's no time like the present."

"Oh really, Rose," Faye admonished, "That's none of our business. We'd better leave, now!"

"Not before I see a dead person," Rose insisted.

"Oh, just be quick about it," Faye answered, "Ruth and I will wait out by the door.

She tiptoed toward one of the forms covered in white. She didn't know why she was tiptoeing as they certainly could not hear her. Maybe it was something about being dead that made others want to sneak around and not be noticed. She stood next to the bed, grasped the top of the sheet and gently turned it back. First the black hair appeared, then the top of the head. She stopped, looked over to the other two and they were shaking their heads. One more little turn back of the sheet and she would see the rest of the face. The eyes were closed and there were bruises around them. The face had a black beard and Rose could just make out the lips that were now a bluish color.

She stared at those lips and realized that once upon a time they would have been moving, perhaps laughing, or telling someone a special story. Those lips would tell this man's history, his name and where he lived. But now they would be forever still. In thirty seconds Rose could see the beginning and the end of this man's life and wondered so much why he was lying here motionless and cold. A shiver ran through her and she took the sheet and covered his head again. She turned and quickly returned to the other two who were waiting impatiently.

"Are you satisfied, Miss Nosey?" Faye asked. "Can we go now? I've had enough exploring for today."

"Yes, yes," Rose answered in a whisper, "I've never seen anything so mysterious and frightening at the same time....but yet there was also a sense of peace. How strange. I don't understand..."

"Let's just go, Rose," Ruth urged, "we should get back before we are missed. Ok? Have you had enough scary stuff for one day?"

"Yeah, I'm ready," Rose agreed, "remember, green, yellow, brown, blue...that's the order of the hallways."

"Uh, I don't think so, Missy," Faye laughed, "It was green, blue, brown, and then yellow"

"No, no, girls!" Ruth corrected, "You have it all wrong. There were only three hallways and the doors into the morgue are blue. I guess I had better lead the way out. Remind me to bring a compass along next time!"

Chapter 30

After their supper in the cafeteria, they met with the other AZMU people to discuss what their duties would be. Rose hoped that they would not be split up but so much for hoping; she was assigned Ward C, Ruth had Ward D, while Faye was sent downstairs to Ward B. They were given their starched white uniforms complete with a white hat and a navy blue cape. Each uniform was accompanied by a white full-length apron that sported two large pockets. Their biggest challenge would be to keep these uniforms clean and starched. One advantage of desert life was that the laundry always dried very quickly.

Their patients were the soldiers injured in the last battle against the Turks and Germans. They would find English, Jewish, and Palestinian soldiers plus the odd Middle Eastern Christian. They would find them in all stages of recuperation from those just following surgery, to those almost ready to be sent back into battle.

They were to tend to their wounds and/or surgical sites, encourage them to eat and drink by helping them to do so, and to assist the Dr.'s and nurses in the administering of treatments and medications. Rose was surprised that they would allow these young novices to do so much, but then she told herself that these were desperate times that required every able hand to help. This would be much different than what they had been doing in Jaffa which was to help the mothers and children with treating trachoma and to educate them on sanitation and proper nutrition.

She was ready to handle more responsibility and took a peek into the faces of Ruth and Faye and realized that they felt the same. She, herself, was not sure how she would react when the actual time came to see a wound, or would have to re-bandage an incision; she just hoped that she would not faint. She didn't think she would as she remembered that back home she was the only one who could stand to treat Mr. Tuxedo's various cat fight scars. Some of them were quite nasty and sometimes required a special medicine from Dr. Epstein, usually one that he was willing to let her have and try on a cat. She didn't mind the oozing blood or puss, but how would she react around a human who had just returned from battle with multiple wounds and broken spirits, she just was not sure. Probably after a few weeks of hospital life she would be most impervious to any muck and gore. At least she would hope she would be.

They were to report to the cafeteria in the morning at 5:30 a.m. for their tea, scone, and slice of cheese accompanied by a small piece of fruit, and then hit the Wards by 6 a.m. First they would meet with the Ward's head nurse and then they would be shown around and introduced to the patients there. Some would be lucid and remember their names and others would be enveloped in their pain and confusion and thus think that perhaps they were someone from home just there to visit. It was always their duty to remain calm during any circumstance whatsoever, be it catastrophic or just routine. By 5:25 a.m. the three California girls entered the cafeteria, grabbed their trays and loaded them with their portions of the morning's meal. Quickly they consumed it all knowing that they would need the sustenance to: number 1, maintain enough energy to get them through to lunch, served at 1 p.m., and number 2, maintain an even temperament as they met who knew what horrid moment that lay somewhere before them.

Rose was the first to say it.

"I wish you all the very best morning that this place can give you."

"Here, here, Rose," Ruth smiled.

"And may your patients have patience with their new patient Aides!" Faye cleverly added.

Ruth and Rose laughed and told her to write that in her diary tonight when the day was over.

"Meet you at 1 in the cafeteria," they repeated to one another and then they were off.

Chapter 31

Rose walked down the hall in the opposite direction from Ruth. Ward C was down at the end of the grey-walled corridor. *It's certainly not a very happy color,* she thought, *Looks like what the inside of a fighter ship would be painted, grey and hopefully unrecognizable by the enemy.*

She found Dr. Meissner and Nurse Mindela at the desk just as she walked into the large room. There were two rows of beds on either side of the two longest walls. There was a walkway down the middle of the room with a black stripe indicating the walking area. Each bed was outlined by a black line on the floor and the window above the bed was small, but did let in enough light so that the patient could possibly read a letter or something. Each bed had a curtain that could be drawn around it for privacy. A small table was placed on the same side of each bed lining the walls and it was white with one drawer and an open shelf at the bottom. On top of each table was a glass of water on a small tray accompanied by a small bowl filled with grapes. Most were untouched since the residents of these beds were not interested in food or drink. They needed the coaxing of the staff to remind them that there were reasons back home to not stay depressed, but to do the best they could to speed up their healing. They were reminded daily about their family or girlfriends who were so eager to hear from them and to get them home again.

Some of the patients who were more advanced in their healing would be allowed out of bed to walk, use the bath, or to sit at a table located at the end of the room for a game of checkers or to read a magazine or a newspaper.

Also, tucked down there in a corner, was an old upright piano that had seen better days, no doubt, but was probably a source of joy when someone would plink out some of the pop songs like: *Hinky Dinky Parlez-Vous* or *Oh You Beautiful Doll.* Usually on the weekends a group of locals would come to the wards to lead the soldiers in some singing. Then they would greet each patient with kind words and leave them a single flower on their little white table.

Many wheelchairs were lined up near the entrance of the ward and these were used by the patients who were recovering from broken, maimed or amputated legs. Yes, Rose knew that some soldiers would be struggling with the news that they had lost an appendage while on the battlefield. She also knew that when changing bandages that she must be on the lookout for gangrene.

She had looked up in a medical book what this condition actually was: *"originally from the French: a condition where the tissue decays from lack of blood to the area. The obstruction of the blood flow was caused by an injury or disease.* Initially she thought that it meant that the injury was actually turning green.

But, rather, it was simply rotting and smelling quite bad. The infected area was more likely to be grey than green. The only treatment would be amputation, or a surgery to remove the dead tissue. Sometimes irrigation with a medicated solution could help, but this was not so common.

Rose pinned her AZMU badge on the top of her apron and then followed Rebecca, the nurse who would be training her, into Ward C.

"I've been here a year now," Rebecca said, "and I've come to know every detail of this room. You, too, will start to feel that this is really your home now and as the soldiers come and go you will learn not to form any attachments or their partings can be too painful. You will lose some and others will recover, and still others will continue to struggle with their now altered bodies. It was hard at first, but now I am used to it."

"I can see how that would be true," Rose responded, "I only hope that I will be as positive as you are."

"So here we are. It's time for their breakfast," Rebecca said, "and you will have the honors of delivering the trays, helping the boys to sit up by propping the pillows, and then assisting them with their eating if they need it. Joyce and Abigail will be helping you. Between the three of you, the boys will be covered."

"How many patients are here, Rebecca," Rose asked, "Are all the beds filled?"

"Generally, we roll one out as another is being rolled in," Rebecca looked at Rose, "The ward holds 20; 20 beds, 10 on each wall, and there are days when we are so crowded that we put extra beds down the middle where that black line is. But that hasn't been the case since General Allenby's attack back in January. The Arab boys have been soldiering with the Brits as well, since no one likes the heavy hand of the Turks ruling Palestine anymore."

"Oh, I've been reading the history of the region as we traveled here from California," Rose added, "It seems that this small piece of land has been in the middle of many disputes and in the hands of many rulers. One statistic said that General Allenby is the 34th conqueror of Jerusalem. Somehow that does not sound good for the people, but I think that this could be a turn for the better since Great Britain would be a benevolent and democratic ruler."

"That's what they say," Rebecca nodded her head, "But really, a region that has so many rulers can only become weaker and weaker in terms of independence and military prowess. As you probably heard, it is the Zionist Jews who want their homeland back since the takeover clear back by the Arabs in the 900's. They want to govern for themselves and create their homeland as it was in the days of King David."

"That sounds like a tall order," Rose said, "but I've also heard that a lot of these rulers were after not only the land, but the oil as well. In fact I read that pursuing oil is one of the main causes for the battles, attacks, and ambushes. As long as there is oil in this region, the killing will continue, I'm afraid to say."

"Yes, I feel that you are right with that conclusion, Rose," Rebecca giggled under her breath, "Some say that oil is 'liquid gold', but I maintain that it is 'liquid death', for all the killing it causes in trying to control it."

"Yeah, I see what you mean," Rose put her hands in her pockets, "how can something so ugly and smelly cause so much suffering?"

The first bed they visited was #1. Here was Donald from Bath, England. He had head bandages but said that yesterday was the first time that he had no pain. Rebecca introduced Rose to him, and then they went to bed #2, then #3 and so on.

It was bed #15 that held a young man with dark thick hair and a very black beard. She saw that his eyes were bandaged and his right leg was being swabbed and dressed by Nurse Rachel. Every once in a while she would give him a drink of cool water to help him through this agonizing procedure. But this patient was lying perfectly still through the agony oftentimes evoking the name of Allah undoubtedly to help him through this ordeal. Rebecca whispered that they would come back later when he was more comfortable.

The rest of the beds held soldiers in all stages of repair. Some were eager to get back to the fighting, while others seemed to say in their facial expressions that they had had enough.

Chapter 32

Now that she had met everyone, it was time to get the meal trays from the orderlies who were wheeling them up on large carts from the kitchen or 'mess hall' in the basement. Unfortunately by the time the food had traveled through a very drafty hall, up some stairs and finally to the correct ward, the food would most likely become cold. But that did not really matter to these boys since they were used to eating cold vittles when they were with their troops.

It appeared that the young Arab boy Rose had seen in bed #15 was alone now, no doubt recovering from the ordeal he had just undergone at the hands of Nurse Rachel. She saved his tray for last with the hopes of being able to sit next to him as a comfort.

When she finished delivering the bowls of oatmeal, and helping the soldiers in beds #3, #7,#9,#10 and #17, she felt that now she could approach bed #15. Perhaps his wound had settled down enough so that this Arab boy could take some good American oatmeal. How strange to be in the Middle East and serving them oatmeal that was so Western in cuisine. Maybe he absolutely hated it and dreaded the meals here as they were so foreign to his tastes. She promised that if that was the case that she would try to smuggle in some humus or couscous for him.

Why this sudden interest in bed #15? It simply wasn't that he was a victim of the vicious battlefield, or that he was trying to make sense of his poor world that had been invaded; no, it was the fact that this helpless individual represented an ancient culture that was clashing with another culture which had rendered him helpless.

He clearly needed help and Rose was here for a reason. She wanted to rub shoulders with his world and what better way to do it than over a bowl of oatmeal. She had decided that she would make bed #15 her project. First, though, she needed to find out everything she could about him. Then, she needed to learn some Arabic...maybe he knew a little Hebrew or English and that would be a help but she wanted to greet him in a tongue that he felt comfortable with; one that would make him feel that he would try to talk to this very white and freckled skinned girl that refused to cover her head and face as was the custom in his world.

She needed to bridge a gap with him that might be impossible to bridge...however Rose never allowed that word into her vocabulary: *impossible*. With Rose, once that word was uttered then the game was on and she meant to have victory over it. *I guess I had better learn his name; that would be a good starting place. Ah, a name...what is in a name...so much, dear Rose, so much you dear young thing whose only world has been the cloistered little berg of Chico, California. Well, all of that is about to change, so hang on, this could be a bumpy ride!*

"And I'm ready for it!" she said aloud.

"What did you say?" Nurse Rebecca turned around, "Did you ask a question?"

"Yes," Rose answered, recovering quickly, "What did you say the fella's name is in bed #15?"

"We're not sure yet," Rebecca shook her head, "We are still looking for that piece of information. Usually we find out when a family member or a friend comes in for a visit. This one is all alone. No one has come to visit.

"He is what we label as a 'Ward Orphan' and we just refer to him by his I.D. number which is located on his chart. I have it here, um, where is it...oh yeah, #WC 7293168M. That's his name for now. I remember now that the girls refer to him as WC729M for short. They don't like working with him as he is surly and generally rude. The girls have their favorites and he is not one of them. I think he tossed his soup bowl at one of them,so they try to give him a wide berth." *Well, he's my favorite now.* Rose whispered to herself. *He's mine now.*

Chapter 33

Dear Diary,

I'm writing you from Jerusalem now. Ruth, Faye and I were transferred here which is where I wanted to be all along. I'm just dying to see the historical and political hot spots of the city but so far no tourist trips yet. On Sunday they promise to let us out for a bit of a hike through the market. I hope that I can get over to see the Wailing Wall – the only wall remaining of King Solomon's Temple. We'll be chaperoned and watched with an eagle eye as the city is really not safe: there are people angry with the Germans, the Turks, the English, and the Arabs are not happy with the Jews or the Turks, for that matter. It could be dangerous for three pale-skinned girls from California wandering the streets alone. I welcome the chaperone as I'm sure that he will be able to answer many questions about the city that I have been storing up in my brain.

We are in the Rothschild Hospital which is quite large. We are helping the soldiers (all of them – enemy or friend) to recover from their time on the battlefields. Most are very grateful for anything that we do for them, but some are somewhat surly, I imagine, from their pain, fear and loneliness. We try to comfort them as well as provide conversation, if they speak English of course. Otherwise, we just smile, try a few hand motions and hope for the best. My Hebrew has improved as I am finally using it, but I also need to use Arabic, German, and sometimes French or Italian. I've picked up a few words here and there, but my ability to mix up the languages is quite common and the soldiers are laughing. I guess amusing them is a good thing, too.

But Diary, I really want to tell you about the Arab boy in bed #15. That's all we know about him right now. He's blind and has a serious leg injury. We hope that it will not have to be amputated. One of my jobs is to cleanse the wound and change the bandage. It is painful, I can tell, as he grabs at the bed sheet twisting and turning it in his fingers. He will not make a sound, but I can tell that he is in a lot of pain.

None of the other girls like dealing with him, but I don't mind. I volunteer to do their chore just so I can get to know him. Actually, I want him to get to know me so that he will not be afraid. He's very angry right now and has grabbed at anything to throw at me. But one thing he does let me do is stroke his forehead. Evidently the shrapnel hit his leg and then bounced up to his forehead but not before landing a piece of it in his left eye. He has been in bandages covering his eyes so he has no idea what is going on around him. He hears a lot of foreign tongues and I am sure that all of this has him spooked. To make matters worse, he is a Ward Orphan which means that no one has come to see him. That's why we do not know his name; just his I.D. number: WC729M. I just call him '729'.

But Diary, this is what I want to say tonight. Today was a great day for me and 729. At least it was for me. I had just finished tending to his leg wound and I was covering him up with the sheet. We are having a heat spell, so I didn't want to make him too warm, but I was sure that he would want to be covered up so as to hide his injury. I gave a couple of strokes to his forehead like I usually do and he reached up, took my hand off of his head and put it to his mouth and then to his heart. I think he was trying to gesture to me that he was thankful for what I was doing for him. I really do. I've told him that my name is 'Rose' but I'm not sure that he understood that...but, Diary, today he spoke my name. In a broken tongue he said my name. At least I think he did, no, he really did. I'm sure of it.

It's these little breakthroughs that keep me motivated to work with him. I don't know anything about him but somehow that doesn't really matter. He's alone, scared, and probably very angry.

Ruth is in Ward D and said that her patients are mostly English. They were fighting the Turks in the last battle here in Jerusalem. They succeeded in pushing the Turks back so now it's just the English, Canadians, Aussies, Arabs and Jews that are in the city. She said that the boys are sweet enough but that there are a few that are depressed due to their injuries. This seems to be a common theme here: loss of limb, depression, and then anger. The really angry gents are carted off to another ward where they can learn to control their emotional out bursts. That would seem to me to be an almost impossible task after coming off one of these bloody battlefields they have had to endure.

Faye is down on Ward A where all the patients are initially placed. They are brought there first and then evaluated as to their backgrounds, nature of the injuries, and how critical they are. Ward B is the one for the critical injuries so some are sent there until they are stabilized. 729 was there for a few weeks I was told. His head injuries were such that his survival was precarious and needed 24 hour care.

Since I've arrived I haven't had a chance to even step outside so I don't know really where I am or what the city is like. If all goes well we should be the tourists from California on Sunday.

Tomorrow I will write home with my new permanent address and I hope that I will get some news from them in a week or so...maybe longer since this is a war zone.
I can't believe that I just said that: 'war zone'. I'm really in a war zone and I had better make note of that as I am in the middle of something spectacular...albeit dangerous, but truly horrifically amazing.

My eyes are closing and in just a few hours I will be back on Ward C. So, sweet dreams for now.

Chapter 34

As the girls settled into their new routines, they also became more abreast of the tragic conditions plaguing the poor of the city. Jerusalem's most pitiful sight was its little army of orphans and abandoned children. Their mothers were either dead or too feeble to care for them and their fathers were lost somewhere behind the Turkish lines.

One such little guy was Yitzhak. An AZMU doctor found him roaming the streets, emaciated and blind, begging for bread. When the air turned cool, Yitzhak knew it was evening, so he fell where he stood and went to sleep, to be awakened by the sun the following morning. He managed to stay alive because he was a familiar figure on the streets of Jerusalem and people saved crusts for him. The doctor picked him up and took him to the Rothschild Hospital where he was cleaned, fed, and pampered. Faye was the first to meet Yitzhak as he was brought into Ward A first.

One afternoon she asked him if he wanted more bread. *No, no, I just want to see again.* Sadly, Faye had to tell him that they were unable to make him see again. But, she promised that they were trying to locate his family. This seemed to cheer him into a smile. When he was transferred to the Children's Ward he seemed to settle in with the other waifs who were recovering from malaria, meningitis, typhoid and trachoma. Immediately Faye put in a request to work with the children. She felt that working with these helpless ones was where she could do the most good.

Ruth stayed on Ward D and enjoyed helping the English who were so easy to joke and kid with. There were nights when the girls met for dinner in the cafeteria and she would be sporting a British accent and retelling the funny stories she had heard rumbling around the ward that day. It appeared that Ruth would become the one to keep everyone's spirits elevated.

Rose would report on the little successes she was having with 729. She was noticing that he had identified her steps now and would turn his head towards her as she approached bed #15. His pain had lessened but he was still not eating and was becoming weaker and weaker. Rose mentioned that the next time they were out that she would make a point of bringing back some Arabic food that might entice him to eat. He definitely was not adjusting to the menu of the hospital.

"I've been reading to him now," Rose mentioned.

"Really?" Ruth asked, "What can you read to him that he would understand?"

"Oh, that's easy," Rose answered, "I read poetry with lots of expression in my voice and it seems to calm him. One time I was reading Elizabeth Barrett Browning and he actually fell asleep!"

"Oh, was that the poetry or your terrible reading!" Faye laughed.

"That's right," Rose said, "I really don't know but I'm saying it was Elizabeth's meter and not me at all!"

On Wednesday the following week the nursing world suddenly came to a halt when the three girls woke with their faces dotted with red spots.

"Ruth, look at me!" Rose screamed, "I have the measles!"

"Well, if you have the measles, so do I," Faye said grabbing the hand mirror. "What is this? I don't feel sick, and I think you are supposed to feel ill with the measles, even run a fever in most cases. Wait a minute, I've already had the measles when I was five. What *is* this stuff!"

"I don't have any idea, but I don't think we should be helping any patients today'" said Ruth.

"You are right. We need to tell Rachel that we need a doctor now," Faye concurred.

"I'm not going to let a few red dots stop me from seeing 729. He would be disappointed if I did not show up," Rose said defiantly.

"Would you rather give him what could be a nasty disease instead?" Faye asked, "Really, Rose, sometimes you just don't think."

"Ok, I'll see the doctor, but no matter what, I'm going up to see my Arab boy, and I don't care what anyone says. My first thoughts are of him and his recovery, not of me and this little red stuff visiting my skin. I think it will all be fine," Rose argued back.

"I wish Father was here," Faye said forlornly, "he would know right away what to do. Oh why is your Father not here when you really need him!"

Dr. Kaplan was free to see the girls and determined immediately that the red dots were from sand flies.

"Sand flies!" he said, "And don't be too hard on them because they haven't had the pleasure of such well-fed animals in years!"

"Sand flies? That's it?" Faye exclaimed incredulously, "Here I've been feeling sick for nothing...I thought for sure that I had a fever! Yes, I *do* feel feverish and I wasn't able to eat breakfast for a rumbly tummy."

"Well, I think that was just your nerves telling you that probably you had some deadly tropical infection," Ruth laughed.

"Just in case, let me feel your head and check your glands," Dr. Kaplan said reassuringly. Faye really did look a bit pale and he confirmed it by asking her to come down to the nurse's infirmary. "No sense taking a chance with malaria and typhoid everywhere."

It turned out that Faye had contracted *enteritis, or gypsy tummy;* A condition that cropped up in sanitary-poor conditions. With Faye out of commission for a couple of days, Ruth and Rose split up her Children's Ward duty between them so they were working extra-long days between them. From then on all the AZMU personnel were required to chew quinine tablets daily. This was to help stave off the malaria threat.

Rose did her research and found out that malaria was caused by a female mosquito biting someone who already had the disease which was caused by a parasite. The parasite most likely was living in dirty water or unsanitary conditions. The parasite lodged itself in the liver and eventually ruptured thus releasing more parasites that infect the red blood cells and causing chills, fever, and nausea. The only precaution available was to stay away from stagnate water and to cover one's skin so as to prevent mosquito bites. After she closed the book on the subject, Rose decided that she would now wear a hat with netting on it to protect her face from the mosquitos. She even vowed to wear it whilst she slept. She didn't care how silly it looked.

With her polka-dotted face, Rose arrived on Ward C ready to tend to her patients. She checked the chart of 729 and saw that he had spent a restless night calling out someone's name, perhaps reliving some nightmare that continued to haunt him.

She went to bed #15 and gazed down at his face that was holding a grimace that was so tight that it could strain the muscles in his neck. She touched his hand and he grabbed it and held it over his heart. She gently touched his leg to let him know that it was time to change the dressing. He shook his head and patted the bed for her to sit. The nurses were not supposed to sit on the patient's bed, but Rose did it anyway. True to her style, if there was a rule she did not find convenient to keep, she usually broke it.

"Rse,Rse," he muttered softly. This was the signal that she had been waiting for. This morning she had found a rose growing out on the Nurse's Patio and she had cut off a bloom. The bush had reminded her of Mother's beautiful rose garden and all of a sudden she felt a pang of homesickness. Now she was going to put this red rose under his nose so that he would know that her name was this beautiful aroma.

She passed the rose under his nose and then said her name again. "Rose, Rose, Rose".

He smiled and said, "Rose!" Now he knew who she was. She kept tickling his nose with this beauty until he sneezed. Then they both laughed aloud.

Then he became serious and took both of her hands in his and said, "Akhil, Akhil."

Rose was certain that he was finally telling her his name. She laughed with joy and said, "Akhil, Akhil, I am so glad to meet you!"

She took his hand and held it up to her face so that he could feel the big smile there. Finally, she knew his name. She guessed that probably there was not too much more to know about him.

Akhil...such a good Arabian name. Well, I guess it is Arabian. He's not Jewish, and they said that he was an Arab, but maybe no one really knows. Maybe he's an orphan from the streets just as he is here on the ward.

For the next few minutes they lightly conversed with Rose saying the few words she knew in Arabic and he trying a few English ones. It would have been easier if he could see for then she could draw him pictures of things and tell him the English word for them. Then he could do the same in Arabic. For now, though, they started with the things that he could feel, touch, smell or hear.

Today she brought in the Rose, yesterday it was an orange but it was a difficult word for him to say. It mostly came out: 'rnj', but that was ok, she knew what he meant. Then he told her the word in Arabic and when she tried to say it, he laughed. *bortoqal* she tried to say only it came out: *bordocall,* not nearly as nice as when he had said it.

Her signal to leave him was a wiggle of one of his toes from the foot of the bed. Now she grabbed it, gave it wiggle and went on to visit her other patients. By the time she had finished her rounds, it was time to bring in the mid-morning fruit trays. Today there were dates and almonds placed in little glass bowls and placed on the white tables beside the beds.

When she got to Akhil's bed (she would no longer call him #729 or bed #15) she gave the signal that she had come back by wiggling the same toe. He smiled and lifted a hand toward her. She put the little bowl in his hand and let him feel what was there. He held up the date and Rose identified it. He took a bite and recognized the flavor and went back for more. Evidently dates were a favorite of his. He smiled and said, *tamar, ah tamar*!

"Oh, *tamar*," Rose parroted back, "I can say that one pretty good!"

He felt into the bowl and found the almonds and then said, "*Looz! Tamar, Looz!*"

"*Looz – almond,*" Rose repeated back to him. "*Looz, Tamar*: almond, date!" Then she took his free hand and stroked his tummy saying, "Yum! good!" He laughed and copied her, "Yoom! goot!"

Chapter 35

My Darling Rose,

We received your letters from Jaffa and Jerusalem and they both arrived on the same day. We understand that the postal service can be quite erratic, but I think they are doing a fine job in that we have received anything from you at all.

Mother asked me to write this first letter to you as she has gone to San Francisco to meet the ship that is carrying Mark. In fact, both she and Bertha left yesterday on the train. You see, Rose dear, Mark was caught in cross-fire and suffered severe injuries. We have been quite upset about all of this but now that we have received word that he is on his way home, things have settled down a bit. We are happy to have him back home, but we do not know the extent of his injuries. We only know that they were serious enough to send him away from the Western Front.

Mother and Bertha will stay at Uncle Walter's in Oakland for a while until he is feeling up to a train ride back to Chico. After he is settled, I will send you an update on his condition.

I know that this will come as a shock to you so I hope that you can find comfort in your friends, Ruth and Faye, being there with you.

Other than this sudden turn of events, the Dupen family of Chico is doing well. Sam and Adam have checked in with letters from time to time, and so far, they are doing alright. Of course, we hope for this terrible war to end soon, and we are hoping it will be before the end of this year, 1918.

Elizabeth and Johnny, of course, send their love and the children have pictures that they have included for you. You will see that they have acquired a new dog, 'Brownie', who is really quite a fella.

Business is good; my arthritis is always good in the summer; and Mother is busy with the Hospital Auxiliary Board, although when she returns she will be involved with Mark's recuperation. Bertha continues to help Mary and Susan at the Blind School and all is well there. School has started and their residents have grown by five. Soon they will run out of room.

And now to your escapade of running away to Palestine with the Epstein's; I have saved this subject until the end.

As you can imagine, Mother and I were greatly troubled by your actions. You defied us and selfishly embarked on this adventure of yours to the Middle East. You have surprised us with your 'cheekiness' many times over the years, but never have you outright defied us and run away from home. Now that you are 18 and graduated from high school, as your parents, we feel that our parenting has probably come to an end. We expect you to support yourself now with some kind of a career and when you return to Chico, we will have a lengthy discussion about what all of this means. If you wish to have more schooling, then we are prepared to discuss this possibility.

This is all I desire to say on this matter. We accept your apologies and we hope that you will return in good health and with many exciting stories to tell us.

With all good wishes, my dear Rose,
Father
Chico, California
September 1, 1918

Rose held on to the chair as she read the part about Mark. She felt like a knife was stabbing her in the stomach. When she had said her farewells to Mark in Liverpool, she had a feeling of dread in the pit of her stomach. Now she knew what that was from. Yes, in just a few months he was injured on the battle front. *Oh Lord, get him home and safe in the arms of Mother and Father.* She cried out in her head.

Never had she felt so disconnected from her family as right now. She realized that if she was to keep up with her antics of wanting to gallivant around the globe following one hot spot after another that she would have to make a sacrifice – a huge one that she would not be near her family when situations like this would occur. Would it be worth it?

Mark was her twin and anything that affected him most assuredly affected her as well. That came with the territory of being born a twin. It was real. She was feeling the pain and agony he was feeling right now.

Oh Mark, whatever happened to you I am feeling it. I don't know what it is, but I know that I am feeling it. By now you should be home, back in your own room. Mother and Bertha will see to you and nurse you better than any military hospital. I'm so glad that they have let you go home. Oh my, oh my! I wish I could use a telephone and call home. Tomorrow I will see about sending a telegram. That surely will speed things up and you will know that I am there with you. Yes, tomorrow I will send you a telegram.

Chapter 36

Akhil was eagerly waiting for Rose. She was hurrying to help him with his first day of physical rehabilitation. They had taken off the bandages from his eyes, and now that his leg was healing, he was being put into a rehabilitation program to help him walk with his crutches and to begin his lessons in Braille. Rose would help him with his transition to Braille since she knew some already. She had told him that her sister (Martha) was blind. Not long after, he would then be fitted with an artificial leg. Yes, they could not stop the gangrene so the amputation took place quickly late one night when Rose was not there.

He was scared even though they had an interpreter there for him. They had finally located one who was willing to enter this western-style hospital. He said that he did not know Akhil or his family but offered to find out as much as he could about him, his friends, and any family members that might still be in Jerusalem.

Akhil had told him that he had not seen his family for many months; that they had become separated after the arrival of General Allenby. The fighting that had incurred caused him to move underground and to stay anonymous. Since he had joined forces with the Arab rebels against the Turks, all ties to anyone he knew were cut.

He then led raiding parties against the Turks until he unluckily backed into a trap and was found defending himself against a Turkish raiding party. If it were not for a band of Brits combing the area, he would not have survived the brutal beating they were inflicting on him.

They wanted information about the British plans and he refused to talk. He not only refused to give them what they wanted, but he tried to show them how much he despised them. At one point he actually spit at the ground in front of them, which constituted an act of defiance and hate.

And now, he was suffering for his boldness with the loss of his eyes and one leg from below the knee. It was worth it. The Turks had raided their village, taken the women, belittled the old men, and threatened even worse consequences if they did not tell them where the rebels were hiding. No one would comply with their threats which made them even angrier. It was like dealing with a rabid dog; the best one could do was to put it out of its misery and kill it. That's what Akhil had decided to do. He would fight and kill as many Turks as he could.

But then there was this sweet girl who had been faithfully visiting him and tending to his needs. She was English, or something. She did not have an English accent, so she was from another country; possibly America, although he could not imagine an American girl choosing to come to a place of such poverty, danger and pestilence. Since the war started he had witnessed the demise of his beloved and beautiful homeland. She had chosen to come here when Palestine was at its worst. He had to admire her for that. Soon he would be wheeled away to the other part of the hospital for his rehabilitation program. He wondered where Rose was. Would she not be able to make it today? But she had promised. It was not like her to break a promise.

Rose was like no other girl he had met. She was fun, eager to learn his language, kind, and caring. He liked to think that she liked him too and that was why she was so devoted to him. He could not see her so he had no idea what she looked like but she said that she wasn't too tall, had an average face and had bright red hair.

Red hair; now that was something new to him. What would his mother think? Ah his mother, where was she? It had been so long since they were together. He missed his brothers and sisters as well. But since he was the oldest, it was his duty to fight against this oppressive enemy and claim their land back. It was a good thing that the British were helping as they furnished the necessary ammunition and other supplies that were needed for these attacks that they made.

One night they had snuck into one of the Turk's camps, wired their fuel garage with TNT and set it afire. That was a spectacular sight, albeit, a bit dangerous to be anywhere near it.

Yes, Rose was the flower he looked forward to everyday. She had started to read to him from a book of poetry, it sounded like. It had a lilting, rhythmic sound and the music of her voice always calmed him. After all, losing part of a leg and his eyesight were mighty disturbing. He experienced many nightmares from all of this and he would often wake up in a sweat and with the thought that he was being pursued and all of a sudden his legs would not move anymore.

Rose, when will you come? When may I hear your lovely voice again?

Chapter 37

"I'm here, Akhil, I'm here," and Rose wiggled his toes to let him know that she indeed had arrived. "I know I am late, I'm sorry. I have bad news," and she took his hand and put it up to her eyes so that he could feel the tears.

"No! No! Why?" Akhil was able to ask in his thick Arabian accent.

"Ahhc," (brother) she simply said.

"Oh, oh, oh," he whispered in shock. "No, no, no, Rose, no."

He sat up and took her face in both of his hands and gently kissed each eye as if he was kissing away the tears. She held on to his hands and pressed her head into his chest. She felt his comforting heartbeat and smelled the hospital scent upon his bed clothes. She suddenly began to sob, quietly, but as if she finally let herself feel the pain and fear she had kept inside for the last two hours. Akhil took his right hand and stroked her head while his other hand still held her head next to him.

She realized that his shirt was becoming wet with her tears so she lifted her head and stroked his cheeks and beard in a manner that let him know that she was grateful for his comfort.

"Thank you, thank you," she whispered. "I'm glad you are here."

"Ahem, Rose, time for us to take Akhil up to Rehabilitation," she heard a voice. And then under her breath the voice said, "Really, Rose, people are watching. You don't want to get reported. Get off of Akhil's bed."

"Right, sorry. It's just that I've only now heard that my twin brother was wounded. I seemed to have fallen apart when I saw Akhil here wounded like Mark might be. What if he is blind as well? I just can't bear to think about that."

"Get a hold of yourself, Rose. We all face tragedies of one kind or another. This is a war that we are in the middle of. Some are here today and then gone tomorrow. Remember, Miss California, this is not some Hollywood movie where everyone ends up happy. Now c'mon and take Akhil upstairs."

"Yes, you are right. I'm usually pretty tough but this really hit me hard. Of course Mark was in harm's way. I just never thought...I'm sorry, it won't happen again. I'll take Akhil now."

"Ok, but be careful. I can't keep covering up for you. As it is, you come here all hours of the night to see him. There's talk. You can't be getting involved with the patients and especially an Arab."

She turned and helped him into the wheel chair. He took her hand and kissed it, "ok, ok, yes?"

She answered, "Yes, yes, ok, ok."

And she wheeled him out the double doors and into the hallway leading up a ramp to rehab.

Chapter 38

The plain truth was that she could not think about too much other than Mark and his injuries and her growing bond with Akhil. She understood the former but was confused about her feelings regarding the latter. She did not know who she thought about the most. Certainly her brother should take precedence over Akhil, but there were times when he did not. Yes, there were times when he did not and that was scary.

Akhil's progress with Braille was encouraging and it seemed that he relied on Rose more and more to guide him. She was pleased that he was trying to accept his two afflictions: a lost leg and lost eyes. How could anyone endure this much tragedy and pain? Plus he had no idea where his family was or if they were even alive. This pained Rose as well so she talked with the interpreter about trying to locate them but he was at a loss as well. Besides, he was sensing that Rose was taking more of an interest in Akhil than was acceptable. He tried to warn her that anything more than a nurse-patient relationship would only bring her heartache. Rose was oblivious to this since she was not privy to the ways and the standards set forth for the women of Palestine. Such relationships with foreigners were shunned and many were trying to warn her of this reality.

Unfortunately, when your heart says something different, you block out all other messages. The message of 'forbidden' held no ground for Rose what-so-ever. She only knew that she just needed to be more discreet about her 'Akhil meetings'.

Ruth and Faye knew about Akhil and had even gone with Rose to meet him. They understood how she felt connected to him and now that Mark had been injured, she was beginning to substitute her feelings of remorse for him with being extra attentive to Akhil.

Thus, they noticed that she was spending less and less time with them doing their usual, 'girl things', and more time reading to him, drilling him on his Braille, and helping him to find his lost family. Her reports of her days were becoming one dimensional now with stories about him and his progress or what funny English word he tried to say that day.

They were concerned and tried to caution her, but to no avail. By now, the end of September, they were leaving the subject alone. They had tried to warn her but decided that their friendship would soon be jeopardized if they did not back off. Still, it was hard to stand back and watch your good friend enter into folly and heartbreak.

It was 4 p.m. and Rose had finished her rounds early. She hurried to Akhil's bedside, wiggled his toes, he laughed and said, "My Rose; my Rose here."

She sat down in the chair, since sitting on the bed was no longer permissible and asked him if he wanted to go outside into the garden, "Go? Go out? Sun? Yes? 'Hellwa' (beautiful)."

"Oh, yes. Hellwa, yes! Sun. Rose, yes."

She found his robe and crutches and they headed for the open doors. They made a left toward the garden instead of a right which led up to the rehabilitation room. His maneuvering of the crutches was improving every day as long as he had Rose there to guide him.

As they approached the garden they could smell the freshness of the grass, the asters, feel the warmth of the sun, and hear the song birds frequenting the hanging feeders. There were a few houses on poles that invited families from time to time, especially in the spring during nesting time.

Akhil stopped, took a big breath in and then let it out with an expansive smile across his face. Rose led him over to a wooden lounge chair that looked like it would be comfortable enough for the two of them.

She saw the jubilation in his face as he tried to angle it toward the sun so that he could receive the full effect of the rays. He pictured himself absorbing these mighty healing beams from the sun that could miraculously restore his sight, or so he wished. He wanted to see this 'hassana' (beautiful girl) Rose, who he was falling in love with.

He wondered if she had the same feelings for him. He wondered, but really he knew. He could tell. They were both in love with each other and about to embark on a most unacceptable trip down love's rocky road. He knew more than she that their feelings for each other would be rejected by both her people and his, but since he was injured and she was his nurse so far the relationship appeared to be professional. He knew that they would have to work at keeping up appearances in that direction but then they would steal a few moments here and there where they could express their true feelings.

Like now; like here in this beautiful garden.
He reached for her hand and stroked her palm while he whispered, "Hassana, hassana, Rose."
She snuggled close to him and said, "'Gamil', Akhil, 'gamil' (handsome).
"*Heppy*, Rose?"
"Yes, I am happy, Akhil; very happy."

She wondered if they were being watched by some nosy ones looking out the window, but she did not care. Not in the least. She had never felt this way before and she was not going to let anything come in the way of it. Not today, not ever. She knew everyone was warning her that affections were inappropriate just as Akhil's interpreter friend was warning him. Neither one of them were paying attention. The rest of the world could disappear for all they cared. Their love was spanning cultures, oceans, religions, and wars.

She had no idea what the future would bring and she just couldn't think about that right now. She was here now with someone who needed her help and she wanted to give it. Otherwise she would feel helpless in the face of this horrible monster, the Kaiser. It was, after all, the Kaiser who had put her dear brother into the hospital. She still did not know what his injuries were. The mail was interminably slow and all she wanted was to know what was going on at home and how he was doing, what exactly happened, and what his future was going to be with his recuperation. She knew nothing of it all, but she did know that she was here now, in Jerusalem, where so many needed her skill and support.

Besides her nursing duties in the hospital, she also accompanied Ruth and Faye and other nurses and doctors to various outlying towns. The more areas that were liberated from the Turks, the more the AZMU group was called upon to bring help. Its members even traveled south to Hebron, the most orthodox Moslem town in all of Palestine.

Just last week they were picked up at dawn in a Ford tin-lizzie crammed with medical and surgical supplies and basic food items. It was only 25 miles to Hebron but it took two hours to travel the distance.

On the way they passed the "Oak of Abraham" a tavern that was owned by a bearded one-eyed ogre of a man. They had been told about Hemmet from others who had traveled this way. Evidently if a traveler did not stop for some of his coffee, then his men, hidden down the road, would ambush them. They had learned the hard way and had spread the word to inform others.

So, this morning, the travelers in the tin-lizzie stopped and partook in some very sickeningly sweet coffee in order to avoid an ambush down the road.

Once they arrived in Hebron, they found that the dilapidated, tumbling town of stone houses and narrow crooked streets was wreaking with disease and lack of sanitation. They ended up treating more Arabs than Jews for the common ailments of malaria and trachoma. Unfortunately, the Jewish hospital had been stripped of every movable item by the retreating Turks.

After a long day, they finally headed back to Jerusalem. They could have spent the night at the Oak of Abraham Tavern but decided that they would risk driving that treacherous ,windy road back to Jerusalem in the dark so as to avoid seeing that onerous Hemmet again.

Chapter 39

More and more new areas were opened and liberated by General Allenby and his Brit soldiers. As the Turks and Germans retreated, however, they left a wake of disease, pestilence, tainted water and rotting bodies on the sides of the roads. The evidence of the war was everywhere. Most recently an epidemic of cholera had erupted and doctors and nurses hurried to these areas to set up Hadassah clinics. Sometimes the AZMU was mistaken for Germans and needed to clear themselves before the British officers.

These efforts to help the liberated towns offered horror as they would see corpses laying in the very water the villagers were drinking. Dogs were seen scratching at the shallow graves only to pull out the dead as their sustenance. The population was afflicted with so many disorders that the AZMU felt that they could only barely scrape the surface to treat them all.

Rose, Ruth and Faye did not go out on any other missions after their trip to Hebron. They were needed in the hospital and the professional nurses were called on to accompany the doctors to these dangerous areas.

Therefore their duties doubled and tripled to cover the loss of manpower. Rose's patient list grew twice the size and thus limited the time that she could spend with Akhil. It was at this time that she would simply spend her sleeping hours with him. That is, she decided to spend the nights with him at his bedside. She did not mind if she had to sit up in a chair all night. She just wanted to be with him. Was this a good idea? The thought crossed her mind which she quickly dismissed. It was a great idea because she would get what she wanted, even if it was for a short while.

The first night went well. She arrived at midnight and then left at 5 a.m. to assume her spot in her own bed. No one knew that she had spent the last 5 hours somewhere else. If anyone noticed that she was gone, she would just say that she was doing research on the Turkish Empire in the library. She had already checked it out and the doors were never locked. She'll say that she was having trouble sleeping and thought that reading would help. They will think that she was just worried about Mark. They didn't need to think otherwise because she really was worried about him. Without communication from home, her mind was left to wander down any path of fear it wanted.

About 2 a.m. one night Akhil and Rose moved to the lounge area of the ward where the piano, couches and tables were. They sat at a table with some coffee and held hands. No need for words. They knew what each one was feeling. It was easy to see that Akhil and Rose were an item.

"Akhil, my unit will be returning to Tel Aviv in 3 weeks," she whispered, "Rose go home, Akhil."

He looked at her face, wishing that he could see it just one time. "No, Rose, no." and he bowed his head into their clutched hands.

"Rose sad. Akhil sad," she whispered into his ear. She wanted him to have this information as soon as she had received it as it would take a while for the two of them adjust to the idea that they would be forever separated.

Or would they; perhaps she could stay here for a year or two and when things calmed down, she could move on to another adventure. But the whole problem with that idea was that she *needed,* she *wanted* to get home. She longed to see Mark. The fact that he was wounded made her realize that she was not as strong and independent as she thought she was; she was very much attached to her family of crazy and fun-loving Dupens.

She wanted to get back there and after she was sure that Mark was ok, she would then travel to see Sam and Adam...as soon as they returned from the battlefields. She knew they were somewhere in France but had no idea where. After she was good and filled with her family's well-being then she would decide where she was off to next.

Staying in the Middle East would only cause problems since she was white, a female, and connected to an Arab. It was a dead end situation that offered no compromise or solutions. She couldn't believe that she was thinking these thoughts because she loved Akhil so much. She loved his sense of humor, his courage, and his love that he had for her. He truly cared about her well-being and let her know this every day.

For her, Akhil had become an island of 'salam' (peace) in the midst of this ugly war. To see so many maimed, diseased and tragically poor humans every day required some hope of 'al-Hubb' (love) and 'salam'. That was another reason why Akhil and Rose were so much in love. They needed this respite from the horrifying realities of war. She had grown up in the last few months since she left the harbor of New York City and submerged herself in the lives who were victims of this atrocious war.

She saw now that if she chose to live a life of adventure where she was hopping around the globe, she needed to realize that along with the adventure would come grief, shock, pain, and forlorn. If she accepted this reality then her life would be totally hers and no one else's.

"Yes, I'm here Akhil, today and every day until I must go home. You must go home, too. You must find your family and begin living your new life as a victim of this wicked war.

We must know that we did the best we could and had the best we could have for this brief period of time. We must accept this gift of love in the midst of tragedy as just that, a gift from fate that would allow us to survive as an island in the midst of this war. I don't want to leave you, but I think that it's something that we both must face."

Of course Akhil could only pick out a few of the words that Rose, his sweet Rose, was saying. But he knew that by the intensity of her voice and the tears rolling down her cheeks that she was addressing the reality that they could not have a life together. They had found themselves in this situation of sweet, nurturing love in the midst of the war's ugliness and it was saving them from sheer mental anguish.

Farid (his interpreter) had warned him many times about becoming too attached to this *Amerikan* but Akhil refused to listen. Better to feel this love and its great healing power than to feel nothing, desolation and futility which is what he had before she became his nurse. He had changed from an angry, violent wounded soldier to someone who became compassionate, content and hopeful. Rose did that for him. Rose was his medicine. Rose was his life.

Would he give up and resort to anger and violence once again after she leaves? He honestly did not know.

Chapter 40

"Rose, you got a letter from home," Ruth rushed in to the ward excitedly. "Read it, read it! I know that you have been waiting so long to hear about Mark. Hurry, read it!"

"Alright, yes, just let me give Marcus his tea that he asked for," Rose answered back.

"By the way, how is Akhil doing; any news on his family?"

"Well, c'mon over here with me and we will ask him ourselves," Rose said cheerfully. She always loved a chance to stop by his bed. He was not in bed this time, however. Rose looked for him over in the lounge area and there he was at the table with his hands positioned over a board of some type.

"Good, he's practicing his Braille. We'll surprise him." They approached the back of him and Rose grabbed a cotton swab and tickled his ear with it. He swat at it as if it was a fly. This happened two more times until he said, "Rose! You! Rose! Ah, today is now good!"

"You caught me; yes, Rose and Ruth, too!"

"Hi Akhil, remember me? I'm Rose's friend from California. How are you?" Ruth came over to the front of the table.

"Are you good?" Rose jumped in. "How do you feel?" and she stroked his arm. That was their signal for asking how he was feeling. "Any pain today?"

"Good, Akhil good. No, no pain but heart hurt. Rose," as he put his hand to his heart. "Ruth? Hi. Ruth good, yes?"

"Yes, Ruth good today. Ruth good," Ruth smiled. Rose held the letter from home out to Akhil so he could touch it. "Ah, Mark?" he asked.

"Mark, yes."

"Read, Akhil, read."

"Ok. I'll read it to both you and Ruth."

Our Darling Rose,

We received your telegram and it was wonderful that you were able to send it although I am sure that it cost quite a penny. Bertha and I arrived home by train with Mark in tow and now he is nicely settled. He is not in any pain at the moment, but it appears that he is suffering from a condition called, Shell Shock. I guess this has developed among the soldiers who were confined to the trenches. Evidently the continual battle noise, the element of surprise, and the horrible conditions in the trenches can cause some mental and emotional disorders that may leave them with frightening dreams and hallucinations.

We are staying close by his side and Bertha is here reading to him, reassuring him of her love, and talking of the plans that had made before he went away. Some nights we hear him crying and other nights he awakes shouting for his comrades.

His physical condition is improving. I know that you were never able to learn what his injuries were and I am sure that was disturbing not to know. He had a head injury and he took a bullet in his thigh, both of which have healed beautifully. The head injury took the hearing out of his left ear but he has about 50% in his right. The military doctor in San Francisco said that this could heal in time. It is definitely not for sure though. But we are only hoping for the best. And finally, along with the loss of hearing in his left ear, he also lost his left eye. Of course we are so thankful that he can still partially hear and see. So many soldiers are coming home in much worse condition. Soon we hope that his nightmares will stop and he will be able to continue with his accounting duties.

I imagine that you have also seen many harrowing events there in Jerusalem dealing with the poor, battered soldiers. This war has just got to end soon.

Other news: As you know, we do not hear from Sam and Adam too often but when we do we are thankful that they are alive and not ill with some rotten disease like the ones they are getting in the trenches. I've heard that trench foot and trench mouth just rots away the skin and invites the rats in to feast on the dead skin. Stephen and Alfred have written faithfully and we are thankful that they are not at the front lines.

I don't know if you are dealing with this now, but there have been reports of a terrible flu that is taking the young, old and diseased very quickly. Nothing yet in our area and I hope that you have not encountered that over there.

Do you know when you are returning? I would like all my children home as soon as possible. I've had enough of worrying and fretting. Father is noticeably more worried these days as well. We are getting older now and these kinds of shocks we cannot handle so well. I would request that you would be home before the winter settles in.

Please write soon so we can have a few words of yours to hold on to.

With a mother's deep love, Mother
September 15, 1918

Chapter 41

Akhil heard the words in the letter and although he could not understand them all, he knew that hearing from her family would make her want to go back home. Mark was her twin brother and she wanted to be with him. She wanted that just as much as he wanted to see his family again. They were caught in a time-warp that allowed them to have a deep love that stopped the throes of war from destroying them completely. It was a time of joy for one minute but always surrounded by tragedy, loss, and pain.

Akhil now knew what it meant to be a victim. He never saw himself as one before but he knew that his happiness with Rose was only sandwiched in between the horrors of living in a war.

Rose finished reading and Ruth solemnly said, "I've heard of that awful flu. Mother wrote of it in her last letter to me."

"We don't have any cases here, do we?" Rose asked.

"I haven't heard of any, but that could probably change in a day."

Rose looked out the window and allowed her mind to drift. She realized that this was not a safe time for humans all over the world. Not only were there wretched diseases from the battlefields, but now the influenza was reaching epidemic proportions. It would only be a matter of time before the Rothschild Hospital of Jerusalem would become overcrowded with flu victims. Its scope of destruction would run rampant up and down the city streets of every village here or in Europe and America much like a fire swallowing every building or tree in its path. There would be no stopping it. All one could do was to wait it out and hope. The children and the elderly would be most vulnerable and then next would be the fragile soldiers who were overcoming their own afflictions from the war fronts.

She looked over to Akhil and took his hand lying atop the Braille board. He was working on some simple English words and was trying to spell some out for Rose and Ruth.

A...K...h...i...l "Akhil, good!" Rose said

w...a...n...t "yes, 'want', what do you want?"

p...e...a...c...e " 'peace', oh Akhil, we all do; yes, *Salam, Salam.* We must have *salam*," and Rose bent her head and she started to cry. Ruth put her hand on Rose's shoulder and one over onto Akhil's. They became frozen and silent as they pondered the world as they had known it a while ago when their lives were with their families and they tasted the sweetness of peace and hope. Would that ever come back to them or were they lost in a vortex of spiraling lives being sacrificed and destroyed?

Rose continued to spend the nights with Akhil and as his Braille improved so did their communication involving their deeper thoughts. Rose knew that Akhil was the eldest of 8 and before the war was helping to feed them by working in a local business manufacturing olive oil. He did not make a lot of money as the Turks continued to tax the Arabs and their businesses ruthlessly.

It was then that Akhil became part of a rebel group. He saw the possibility of making life better for his family and friends if he stepped up and tried to sabotage the Turks. His dream was to run them out of Palestine. Once the British arrived, this dream started to take form, but then one fateful day he stepped in front of his brother and took the incoming fire to protect him. He knew that they were in hiding now and would not risk coming to the hospital to see him. He felt that soon he would get news from them through Farid. Farid had connections with the rebels and could possibly send a message to them.

Rose used the Braille tablet to tell Akhil that she too was from a large family but that she and Mark were the youngest. She said that she always wanted to see the world and was excited to come with Ruth's family and the medical unit to help the poor and sick. She had a good, safe life in Chico and really could not complain about any of the things that Akhil had to deal with. She also said that she never expected to meet someone that she would fall in love with while on this mission. She was not prepared to have such strong feelings.

Akhil then said that he had been very angry and scared to be in this Jewish hospital. But then he met Rose and his life changed. He said that sometimes life will give you a lemon and that it was up to us to turn it into a sweet drink.

Rose laughed and said that they say that all the time in her family. "When life gives you a lemon, you just have to make lemonade!" Then they both laughed.

They talked about Akhil's future and how he would support himself now that he was crippled. Rose thought that maybe she could contact the Hadassah group to see if they would like him as an interpreter to help with the 'zhondie elyon' (Arab soldiers).

Akhil asked what she would do back in America and Rose said that she would work, write and sell her articles about the war, Palestine and the Jews and Arabs trying to live next to each other, and when she had enough money saved, she would travel again.

He asked if she would want to marry and have a family but she said that her love was here looking at her and if she could not have him, then she would have no one at all. She would, instead, make trips back to Jerusalem to see him. She would give him her address and they would write. He could use the braille typewriter as he was doing now and she would read it, maybe getting some help from Martha, her blind older sister.

Would he want a family?" she asked. He thought the same as Rose and did not see how an Arab girl could take the place of her. But, he was not sure how much pressure his family would place on him to marry so that grandchildren would crown his mother and father. Maybe since he was maimed they would not expect so much from him. His other brothers would have to provide the double amount of children to make up for his shortcoming. They both laughed at this thought!

Rose said that she did not have to worry about providing grandchildren in her family as her older siblings were already providing enough. So far there were 15! She figured that it would make sense that the youngest daughter and the oldest daughter would not marry and reproduce. They would stand as the matriarchal bookends to the Dupen clan.

She said that her parents were older and Father was looking frailer as the days went by. The whole catastrophe of this war left him very worried about his boys who were fighting. And, she suspected, she, herself, had added a line or two to his face.

Akhil's parents were simple peasants who managed a few cows, sheep, and chickens. They worked hard, but with the war, many things had been destroyed including their home. The last he knew, they had moved into the barn where the animals were. Akhil feared for their health there.

Akhil and Rose pledged to stay devoted to each other no matter where life took them. This part was hard to say to each other as they so wanted to build a life together. This dream just could not be in the world as they knew it now.

Chapter 42

Akhil did not feel like eating. It had been since yesterday that he had eaten. But Rose had brought him a lovely, sweet pomegranate and together they devoured it. They said that he had a slight fever so perhaps that was why he was not hungry. They gave him many cups of tea but even that was starting to upset his stomach.

Rose arrived close to midnight and saw that he was sweating on his brow. She alerted the night nurse and they took his temperature and felt his pulse. They were both elevated. Akhil was sick and needed attention. During this last week in September there were already 10 cases of the feared influenza reported in the hospital. It looked like Akhil would be number 11.

They immediately put him on a regimen of aspirin, fluids, and cinnamon milk to help with the fever, and aches. However, his body was not responding and his fever soon topped 105 degrees. He was put into isolation and Rose was only permitted to talk to him from a distance. He was too weak to speak so he would raise his hand and place it over his heart to let her know that his love for her was ever present.

By day 3, cold compresses were added all over his body to control the raging fever. Rose ached and fretted for him. She was obligated to keep up with her rounds even though her love was fighting the worst and deadliest battle of his life.

On day 4, the secondary infection of pneumonia had seized his lungs and he was coughing up blood. Rose begged to see him and finally on day 5 they acquiesced and let her go to his side. They did not expect him to recover and they felt that they should grant this last wish.

They insisted that she wear a mask so as to protect herself, which she did until the attending nurse left his bedside. Then she slipped it off and bent down to kiss his forehead, eyes, and cheeks. He fluttered his eyes, a natural reaction, even though he could not see a thing. But he knew that she had come. He had been calling for her. Finally they found her and led her to him. Now he would get better. Now he had hope. Now he would win this war that was trying to claim his body.

Her tears fell upon his cheeks; his dark, black beard absorbed them. She kept saying his name over and over... "Akhil, Jameel, Akhil, Jameel. I won't let you go. I will stay here forever to be your wife, your love, your heart. I am yours and you cannot die. You just can't I won't let you..." and then she began to sob.

She stayed there all day and all night. She would hide when she heard someone coming into the ward, then return when they left. She applied the compresses, stroked his head and arms, and caressed his hands. She knew that she was taking a chance by exposing herself to this disease, but she did not care. She simply did not want to live without him. She couldn't and she wouldn't. The only way to get out of this mess was for him to get better.

He reached for her and held her tight then he would push her away for fear that she too would become violently ill. Then he would cough and cough and she would be right there to give him water, and stroke his shoulders.

She saw the blood that came up when he coughed. It was frightening as it meant that the nodes in his lungs were now infected. She did not tell him and she was thankful that he could not see it. She just kept reassuring him that within another day all of this would be over. He would be well and ready to eat a big lamb dinner and that she would bring him his favorite; *halvah* (candy).

She cooed and fussed over him, told him stories of home, described the autumn days in Chico and talked about the birds that were out in the garden cheering him onward to health. She said that the British were continuing to push back the Turks and Germans and that soon they would be gone forever. She reported that Farid thought he was getting a lead on the whereabouts of his family and that he would soon get to see his mother and father.

She did not mention that the hospital was filling up daily with more influenza cases and that Hadassah was trying to stay ahead of the epidemic by counseling the people about proper nutrition and sanitation. They warned them of the flu symptoms that would first occur and then gave instructions on how to treat them with aggressive means.

They handed out aspirin until their supplies ran low and then contacted sources in England, and the United States to have more shipped in.

She also did not tell him that darling Faye was now fighting it and that her parents had been contacted and were on their way down from Tel Aviv. Ruth was preparing to go back there to be with her parents as they were concerned that she might contract it from Faye. There was also talk that Rose would return with Ruth but she would not hear of it. She would not leave Akhil's side. She didn't care what happened to anybody right now except for Akhil.

And that is what she did tell Akhil, that she would never leave him. That she would nurse him and make him well. That they would live to see many days together; that their children would have his beautiful black hair with tinges of her red hair to show that they would have some of their mother's spunk. She didn't care if they had 1 child or 20, all she wanted was that he would survive and they would be happy.

She even said that she would be willing to dye her hair black, become a Muslim, cook his favorite Arabian foods, and speak Arabic impeccably. She would promise whatever she could to make sure that he stayed alive. She wanted him now more than ever and wondered how she could have ever thought that she would leave him and go back to Chico, California. What a ridiculous thought that was.

She didn't think about Mark anymore. She knew that he would be fine even if he could see and hear only 50%. Bertha was there to care for him and soon they would be married and Mother and Father could then add more names to their gaggle of grandchildren.

She promised and promised again that she would be a better person, to not be so selfish, to not devise any more escapades, ever again if only, if only...*Akhil...let him live. Oh please. And the tears came again.*

Chapter 43

She awoke to Akhil's erratic breathing that sounded raspy. His lungs were having a hard time receiving the oxygen for all the fluid that was in there. He looked even paler and she tried to rouse him, to awaken him, to stop him from slipping away.

It was day 6 and Akhil left Rose at 5 a.m. He was holding both her hands and then they went limp. She stood up, sat down again, and then bent over to listen for his heart. Yes, it was beating, ok, no, that was the loud pounding of her heart. She grabbed his wrist and felt for his pulse. She couldn't find it. She felt her wrist to make sure that she had the right place on his. She knew how to find the pulse; she had been doing it every day for weeks. Calm down, calm down. There, she had the right place. No it wasn't after all because she felt nothing; nothing at all.

Then it hit her; Akhil was gone. He had slipped away during the dawn of the day. He had slipped away and she could not stop him. He left and now she was alone. She bent over him and sobbed into his chest. Her beloved Akhil was gone and she could not stop that big monster called death. She could not bargain, she could not plead; she could not find a way to save him. She had failed. It was her fault. It was the war. It was her stubbornness. It was the Turks and the Germans, oh how she hated them, and it was the British too who had not done enough. It was the filth of Palestine. It was the fact that the flu was traveling around the world taking whomever it wanted.

Well, she just hoped that it would take her. She wanted to die with Akhil and that was all there was to it. Forget her dreams, her family, and her promises. She would throw all of that away just to be with him.

"Rose, Rose, what has happened. Rose, get up so I can check Akhil. Sit up Rose, you must sit up." The night nurse was standing over her.

Reluctantly she sat up, still sobbing. The attending nurse listened to his chest, stood up straight, patted Rose's head and then pulled the sheet up over his head.

"I will call Ruth for you. You must leave now, Rose. Nothing will change if you stay."

"No, I don't want to leave just yet. I promise that I will go, but just give me a few more minutes. Please, I must see his beautiful face. I must feel his soft beard one more time. Please."

"Alright, I will go out and call the floor doctor and when he comes in, you must leave, understood?"

"Y-y-yes, I understand."

The nurse gave her a handkerchief and Rose wiped her face which had become swollen with the tears. First she felt hot and then she was full of chills. She was nauseous and then she cried again. She thought of her helplessness with Akhil and then she thought that she just wanted to run away out into the desert and disappear forever. She wanted the jackals to find her and devour her body.

No, she could not accept that Akhil had died and she would fight it with all she could. She talked to him and urged him to come back to her, to be her husband. She said that he could do anything he wanted and that he just had to decide to come back. He could do it...he could do...

But no, that did not happen. Ruth arrived, helped her friend up and guided her out of the room. Rose would not return there again. She would keep to her bed for a week and then the Epstein's would take her away all together; away from Jerusalem, away from the hospital, away from her room, away from Akhil's death bed.

Ruth would stay by her side all through the nights and days. Rose would cry, scream, run a fever, refuse food and beg to be left alone to die.

But Rose was strong. She was a fighter. She tried to give up but her strong will would not let her. She had never given up at anything and frankly did not know how to do it.

Oh, she wanted to, that was for sure. The desire was there, but not the will. Her bold character would not let her disappear with Akhil. No, there was too much that was waiting for her to discover, experience, and create in the remaining years of her young life. Eighteen years of age was just too young to write yourself an epitaph...*I died for love, and that's all there was to it.* Personally, she could never tolerate such melodrama and frankly she wasn't going to stand for it now.

It was mid-way across the Atlantic that she realized that she was going home to finish the rest of her life. She had no plans, her hair was dirty, straggly, and her eyes so puffy that she could barely see and to tell the truth, she did not know who she had become and felt like she was a stranger to herself.

Ruth was happy to have her friend back and reported that Faye had recovered from the flu and that no one else had contracted it, including Rose, herself, whom they were very concerned for. After all, laying with the ill can oftentimes lead to death. Her father said that probably she had built up a lot of resistance to that nasty flu just by being as feisty and strong-willed as she was.

It was then that Rose decided to confess and tell the Epstein's, including Ruth, that she had run away from home and that, in fact, she did not have her parents' permission to travel to Palestine; that all of her brothers were fighting the war and they did not want one more over there if it was not necessary. They did not think that having an adventure abroad was worth the dangers at that time. After the war, they promised, she could take a trip to Europe, visit her relatives in England and have a grand time.

Of course, that would just not do for the likes of Rose so she took off, survived, fell in love, wanted to die, saw hunger, pestilence, and poverty and had earned her 'stripes' as a nurse's aide with the AZMU. She had traveled with the Hadassah Zionists and championed the Jews to better living conditions. But then she met Akhil and realized that the Arabs were just as bad off and that what they needed was to get rid of the Turks and the Germans which was happening at this very moment.

It was October 20th and in a fortnight they would land in New York City and not long after that travel back across the many states to California. Winter would want to settle in and she would need some heavier clothes than what she had brought with her so she would shop with Ruth in New York before heading west. She would be able to say to others that she traveled half-way around the world to lose her heart and that now she was back, ready to find it again.

She meant what she had told Akhil. She really would have become his wife and would have been delighted to join his Arab family. She was willing to make that decision because love is the fuel of life. She learned something and that was the fact that love is so powerful that it can cause a person to become another in order to stay in that place of magnificent adoration. She had tasted it and realized that probably she would never feel that again.

Her chance was with Akhil and it lasted for as long as it could, given the circumstances. Isn't that how it is with most everyone else? You stay in love until you can't anymore, for whatever the reason. The fire continues until it doesn't. It is alive until it dies. Hers had died with Akhil's life and she imagined that it would not resurrect itself anytime soon, and, probably not ever. She didn't think that she could handle such intense feelings of passion again; it would probably, literally, kill her. It certainly had almost this time.

She considered herself the wife of Akhil now, and she was able to make sense of it all by saying that he had died in the war, like so many soldiers had. She would join the ranks of widows and at 18 walk the world in solitary.

Epilogue

Rose was right. She never married and always felt that all the love she possessed had been given to Akhil. She had no regrets and, in fact, prided herself with the awareness that regrets really did not serve anyone. Oh sure, she became more sensible, less demanding, but never once did she regret a decision to move on, to see what was around the next corner.

After returning to Chico, her sister Elizabeth hooked her up with a publisher who wanted Rose's perspective on the Middle East, the conflicts there and the hope of the Zionists to settle Palestine as their homeland. In her later years she established herself as a reliable journalist and foreign correspondent. She liked the thrill of travel and continued doing so, well into the 1980's. She even spent time in the White House as part of the press through the Eisenhower and Kennedy years. She was against all war but did volunteer to cover them as they arose. War never proved to be a good or reasonable action to her and she wrote that in her various pieces.

Rose dedicated herself as a volunteer at the Chico hospital upon her arrival home and proved to be quite helpful in treating the Chico residents suffering from the flu epidemic. She remained healthy for the rest of her life until she was 85 years when she fell while ice skating in Switzerland one winter holiday. She had suffered a broken spine and soon contracted pneumonia which united her finally with Akhil. Ruth continued her mother's nursing role alongside her father in Chico. She met Arthur Feldman while in San Francisco finishing her studies. Arthur was in residency at the University of California Hospital and together they decided to travel to Jerusalem with the Hadassah movement to help with the establishment of more clinics. They married there, much to the shock of both of their parents, but managed to calm them down enough to convince them that they were truly in love.

They eventually joined the Epstein Clinic and renamed it *The Epstein-Feldman Clinic*. Arthur specialized in obstetrics and delivered their 5 children, 3 boys and 2 girls. One of the girls was, unsurprisingly, named Rose.

Faye remained in the Sacramento area and married a doctor as well. She kept up on her nursing but opted not to go to school. She was anxious to start a family since her brush with death had caused her to seize the moment and not wait for better times. She tended to run her family's life in an intense impulsive manner because of her experiences in the Middle East. She carried the effects of that journey the hardest and absolutely forbade her children to travel until they were married and on their own. Her 4 boys and 4 girls did eventually marry and leave the area, only to return once in a while for special occasions.

Rose's brothers returned from France and the trenches in reasonably good shape. Mark had the most serious injuries what with the loss of hearing in his left ear, and the loss of sight in his left eye. The following spring, he and Bertha were married and he continued with the CPA firm he was with and then eventually went out on his own as Mark Dupen, CPA. He developed an admirable clientele who trusted his integrity and knowledge of the ever changing tax laws. Eventually he was elected to the Chico City Council. He and Bertha had one daughter, Melanie who later graced them with six grandchildren, three boys and three girls.

Sam and Adam went back to their ranches following the war and continued with their successful cattle business. They were lucky and escaped serious injuries at the Western Front but did suffer a serious bout of the flu on their passage back home. They were sequestered at a military hospital in New York while they recovered and then took the rail back to Chico where the Dupens hosted a welcome home party at Bidwell Park in the center of town.

Stephen and Alfred returned to their families in Sacramento and Los Angeles, respectively. They had not seen actual gun fire during the war as they had been behind the lines as code breakers. They also avoided the flu epidemic only to come home and suffer food poisoning while staying in a hotel in San Francisco.

Historical Notes

The Hadassah Movement

The Hadassah Movement was the dream of Henrietta Szold. In 1909 at age 49 she traveled to Palestine for the first time and discovered her life's mission: the health, education and welfare of the Jewish community there. With six other women she founded Hadassah which recruited American Jewish women to upgrade health care in Palestine.

Hadassah's first project was the inauguration of an American-style visiting nurse program in Jerusalem. Hadassah funded hospitals, a medical school, dental facilities, x-ray clinics, infant welfare stations, soup kitchens and other services for Palestine's Jewish and Arab inhabitants.

Szold persuaded her colleagues that practical programs open to all, were critical to Jewish survival in the Holy Land. Today, there are two Hadassah medical centers in Israel (both in Jerusalem) that are busy, dynamic and vital centers of healing. On average, they treat over a million patients a year and are dedicated to research, education and grant funding for more programs.

World War I

Originally this war was called 'The Great War', 'The War to End All Wars', or 'The European War'.

No one expected another war of this magnitude to occur again, but 25 years later, the world was again engaged in global warfare. Thus the name, World War I and World War II were assigned to each event.

Essentially, it all started when Archduke Franz Ferdinand of Austria was assassinated. He was the heir to the Austria-Hungry Empire. He was killed by a Yugoslav nationalist in Sarajevo. They wanted independence from the Empire but the Empire, in turn, demanded an ultimatum from the Kingdom of Serbia. The Serbians refused and this created a stand-off where eventually the Austro-Hungarians fired the first shot. Because of the treaties set up with other countries, the crisis soon escalated and the allies for each side were soon fighting each other as well.

The war began July 28, 1914 and ended on November 11, 1918. The two blocs of allies were: The Allies (Great Britain, France, the Russian Empire, and later Italy, the United States, and Japan), and The Central Powers (The Austro-Hungarian Empire, Germany and later the Ottoman Empire and Bulgaria).

By the end of the war, the four major imperial powers – the German, Russian, Austro-Hungarian and Ottoman Empires – ceased to exist. A map of Europe was redrawn with several independent nations restored or created.
More than 9 million soldiers were killed.

The Influenza Epidemic of 1918-1919

The flu that reached all corners of the globe took 500 million people – more than the war itself.

The epidemic spread to remote Pacific islands and the Arctic. It has been named one of the deadliest natural disasters in human history.

Many feel that the virus began in the camps of WWI, notably in France. It spread quickly through the soldiers as they were malnourished and their immune systems were compromised.

The symptoms were: high fever, diarrhea, cough, and later pneumonia. Treatments centered on quinine, cold compresses for the fever, aspirin and sometimes, cinnamon milk to help break the fever and, of course, just plain luck.

Printed in the USA
CPSIA information can be obtained
at www.ICGtesting.com
CBHW051519190824
13410CB00050B/1695